AMBUSH

Torn whirled, pushing Crane with his left hand, reaching for the Colt Peacemaker with his right.

Two men were stalking down the alley, side by side, pistols in hand. Torn realized they'd been trying to Indian-up on him, to get as close as possible and make their first shots count.

When they saw the game was up, they started shooting.

Torn heard the hot lead shimmy in the air and slap into the hardpack. He fired and moved at the same time, feeling the breath of a bullet on his cheek.

The alley was filled with a fog of gray gunsmoke. A slug plucked his coattails. He didn't flinch. It was the gunman's last shot. As his hammer fell on an empty chamber, every trace of color bled out of the gunman's face. Torn's Peacemaker barked twice.

Also by Hank Edwards

THE JUDGE

WAR CLOUDS

GUN GLORY

TEXAS FEUD

Published by
HARPERPAPERBACKS

HANK EDWARDS

THE JUDGE

STEEL JUSTICE

HarperPaperbacks
A Division of HarperCollins*Publishers*

HarperPaperbacks   *A Division of* HarperCollins*Publishers*
             10 East 53rd Street, New York, N.Y. 10022

Copyright © 1991 by HarperCollins*Publishers*
All rights reserved. No part of this book may be used
or reproduced in any manner whatsoever without
written permission of the publisher, except in the case
of brief quotations embodied in critical articles and reviews.
For information address HarperCollins*Publishers*,
10 East 53rd Street, New York, N.Y. 10022.

Cover illustration by Darrell Sweet

First printing: September 1991

Printed in the United States of America

HarperPaperbacks and colophon are trademarks of
HarperCollins*Publishers*

10 9 8 7 6 5 4 3 2 1

CHAPTER 1

HE WAS A TALL, LEAN MAN DRESSED IN BLACK. HIS wheatcolored hair was close-cropped, his eyes gray as a gunbarrel. The stage rolling down the Little Rock Road into Fort Smith, Arkansas deposited him at the station on Garrison Avenue. This, the town's main thoroughfare, sloped down to the wharves on the river. At the top end of the old garrison road was a handsome steepled church, shining white in the summer sun.

Clay Torn stood a moment in boardwalk shade and admired the church. Its tapered columns and imposing pediment reminded him of home, the South Carolina plantation house in which he had been born and raised; the house Sherman's looting Federals had picked clean and burned to the ground.

His features grim-set, Torn bent his steps downhill in the direction of the river. The street was wide, bustling, lined with stone and brick buildings. He passed the famous

1

opera house and worked his way through the chaos at Texas Corner, where dozens of covered wagons filled the plaza—emigrants organizing themselves before venturing into the Oklahoma Territory.

From the plaza Torn could gaze out across the wild and beautiful country these people were preparing to brave. The Arkansas River snaked through black bottom land, hemmed in by forested hills. A blue haze veiled distant, rocky bluffs.

By treaty with the Five Civilized Tribes, roads had been hewn out of the wilderness for the benefit of the emigrants, one west to North Fork Town in the Creek Nation, another south to Fort Towson in the land of the Choctaw. They could pass through the Nations, but they could not settle there—the land belonged to the tribes. Other than to charge tolls at bridges along the way, the Indians generally did not bother the travelers. But outlaws often did, and as he slipped through the crowd in the dust-choked plaza, Torn wondered if all these folks would make it safely across the Territory.

Oklahoma was chock-full of desperadoes, bootleggers and brigands of every persuasion. The Five Civilized Tribes were individually responsible for maintaining law and order in their respective Nations. Each tribe had its own lighthorse police, but these units were as a rule woefully undermanned and unable to stem the rising tide of lawlessness. Outlaws knew a good thing when they saw it. In the Nations they were relatively safe from legal retribution, and they pursued their criminal enterprises with impunity.

It was into the Nations that Clay Torn, federal judge, was going.

He carried his few belongings in a black leather valise. A Winchester .44–40 repeating rifle in a scabbard was belted to the valise so that he could carry bag and long gun both with one hand, keeping the other always free. A Colt .45 Peacemaker rode in the holster on his hip.

Crossing Third Street, he entered the less reputable quarter of Fort Smith. Between Third and the river were rundown cabins and rawboard shanties. Sunlight flashed off tin cans cut open, flattened out and tacked over holes and cracks in the warped, weathered walls of the shacks.

Prostitutes, ruffians, river pirates, smugglers—a host of men and women with checkered pasts and precious little respect for law and order—made this part of town one rough neighborhood. Torn felt their wary scrutiny. They watched him pass, looking out from windows, doorways, and sour, trash-filled alleys. Some knew him. Many knew of him. Most were afraid of him.

Those who knew him best knew also that the Winchester and the Colt were not the sum total of Clay Torn's personal armament. Under his black frock coat, carried in a custom-made shoulder harness, was a knife, but not an ordinary knife, by any means. Fifteen inches of tempered steel, complete with single guard bow and bloodtrench, sheathed snug and upside-down against his left side.

Once, the knife had been a run-of-the-mill cavalry saber. Now it was part and parcel of a legend fast taking root on the frontier. From the Red River north to the Canadian border there were folks who knew of a grim, soft-spoken, tough-as-nails judge who made life miserable for the corrupt and the crooked.

Torn's long strides carried him through the riverside quarter, and more than a few of its seedy inhabitants breathed a sigh of relief at his going. He crossed a cobblestone street running the length of the wharves. A peg-legged man with a stern, Puritan face and a beard reaching his beltbuckle was rifling through bills of lading. He looked, thought Torn, like Noah in grimy overalls, as he supervised the work of a half-dozen dockhands loading crates of farming implements and cases of canned foodstuffs onto a riverboat named the *Jezebel*.

"Got room for a passenger?" asked Torn.

"How fur you going?"

"North Fork Town."

"Aye. It'll cost you five dollars. Hard money, up front."

Torn paid. "Not very trusting, are you?"

"What? In this neck of the woods? You must be daft. Captain Gill's my name. Who might you be?"

"Name's Torn."

He cast a dubious eye over the *Jezebel*, stem to stern. She was a sand-river steamer, drew two feet fully loaded, and looked like a cross between a steamboat and a scow. The pilothouse stood between twin smokestacks, and behind the pilothouse was a row of small cabins. She was seeping steam; the fireman had already stoked the boiler furnace. If the vessel had seen better days, mused Torn, they were a distant memory.

"What's wrong?" grated Captain Gill. "Never seen a steamboat before?"

"None quite like this one."

"Despite her name, she's always been faithful. May not look much like a lady, but she ain't busted her belly band yet, and she can slide over a sandbar smooth as a squaw's behind." Captain Gill peered at Torn's somber black attire in a squinty, sidelong way. "You a preacher man, by any chance?"

"Not hardly."

"Thank God. This hyar river is a mean son-of-a-bitch, and she riles me now and again. Ain't got nothing against Bible-thumpers, understand, but when I get riled I've been known to talk up blisters on boot leather. If you ain't no preacher, what are you? You're dressed like a damned undertaker."

"Federal judge."

"That so? Well, there ain't no law to speak of in the Nations, Mister Judge."

"I know," said Torn. "I brought some with me."

C H A P T E R

2

AN HOUR LATER THE *JEZEBEL* WAS LOADED FOR ITS upriver run. Captain Gill cut loose with the steam whistle. His crew fell to work, pulling in the gangplank and casting off mooring lines fore and aft. The paddle wheel churned the river into froth, and the steamer pulled away from the landing. Swinging into the current, she plowed doggedly up the Arkansas.

Captain Gill had invited Torn to the pilothouse. The *Jezebel*'s skipper was manning a high-mounted wheel bristling with spoke handles. Gill pointed out the old fort on Belle Point, now empty.

"The bluecoats are in new forts farther west," explained the riverman. "Gave up trying to stop the bootleggin', which is like trying to stop a prairie fire with your own spit. The Kiowas and Comanches have been herded onto reservations west of the Chickasaw Nation, 'twixt the Red River and the Washita. They've been playing hell with the

Five Civilized Tribes, who are too damned civilized for their own good. 'Course, it's hard to find a full-blooded Cherokee, Creek, or Choctaw these days. Mixed bloods, nine times out of ten. French and Scotch, first off. Then American. They read and write, dress and talk like white men, farm the land, and go to church on Sunday. Sitting ducks for the likes of the Kiowa and Comanches. Yep, too all-fired civilized, you ask me. 'Cept for a handful. The lighthorse police, for example. Those are men you don't want to cross."

"Yes," said Torn. "I can vouch for that. Heard of Big Mike Walker?"

"Sure. The sheriff of North Fork Town. Part Creek Indian, and mean as a mountain lion in a Number Four trap. You a friend of his?"

"I know him."

"I'm glad you're not his enemy—for your sake. He the reason you're going to North Fork Town?"

Torn nodded. Big Mike's summons had caught up with him in Little Rock, via the St. Louis offices of the Tenth Judicial District.

Need help, Big Mike had written. *You're the only man I know I can trust. Come quick.*

Torn had wasted no time. He knew Big Mike as one of the bravest lawmen in the Nations, and if he needed help, then the odds were stacked heavily against him.

Thinking about Big Mike and the circumstances which had brought them together years ago, Torn again looked bleakly into the past. He felt the shape of the daguerreotype he always carried in the breast pocket of his frock coat.

"I guess you've taken a lot of people up and down this river in your time," he said.

Captain Gill gave an emphatic nod. "All kinds. Sam Houston, for one. They called him Big Drunk. He could sure put away the strong-water. Stand Watie. Belle Starr, too. Meanest she-wolf I ever had the misfortune to meet."

Torn showed him the photograph. "Ever seen her?"

Captain Gill took a long look, pursing his lips. "Don't honestly recall. Pretty girl. Who is she?"

"Melony Hancock."

"Wife?"

"Almost."

"What happened?"

"The war. We were engaged to be married. I went off to fight."

"Which side?"

"The Confederacy."

"Good for you. Where is she now?"

"That's what I'm trying to find out. I was wounded and captured at Gettysburg. Spent sixteen months in a prisoner-of-war camp; I escaped in '65. When I got back to South Carolina I found my home destroyed, my family dead, and Melony gone."

"Gone, and you don't know where?"

Torn shook his head, pocketing the photograph. He grimly watched the river rush by. "Rumor had it that Yankee deserters took her. The trail brought me out here to the Nations. That's when I met Big Mike for the first time."

"But you never found your woman."

Torn smiled. *Your woman.* He appreciated Captain Gill putting it that way.

"No. Not yet."

"Been nigh on ten years since the war, but you ain't never stopped looking," marveled the riverman.

"I won't until I find her."

That first day out of Fort Smith they passed the Skullyville landing where, said Captain Gill, the *Jezebel* would stop on the return trip to pick up a load of cotton, harvested by the Choctaw and bound for Arkansas mills. Skullyville was the old Choctaw capital. Its name was derived from the Choctaw word meaning money, *iskulli*.

"And money is one thing the Choctaw know how to make," allowed Captain Gill. "A savvy bunch. The first to come to the Territory. I don't mean to make it sound like they come of their own free will, you understand. The whites wanted their homeland in Mississippi, so the whole tribe got moved out here, and they weren't asked polite-like. Same happened to the Cherokee in Georgia. Heard of the Trail of Tears? That's when the Cherokees were shipped out here. Wasn't a good trip for them. Thousands died. They didn't have clothes or food or weapons to pro-tect themselves with." Captain Gill shook his head. "Bad business. All five of the Civilized Tribes got relocated 'cause the whites wanted their land. Funny part of it is, the whites gave 'em this country 'cause at the time it didn't seem to be worth nothing. Now the whites got other ideas. Reckon sooner or later they'll take the whole Territory away from the tribes. Like I said, too damned civilized for their own good."

The third day found them leaving the Arkansas just below Webber Falls and turning up the South Canadian.

"Sometimes I stick to the Arkansas and go on to Three Forks," said Captain Gill. "That's where the Verdigris, the Neosho and the Arkansas come together, but it's a rough stretch 'twixt here and there. You got to grasshopper over the falls, and then you're smack in the middle of the Devil's Race Ground. An ornery stretch of white water, believe you me."

Torn learned that the technique called "grasshoppering" utilized derricks located at the *Jezebel*'s bow. The derricks swung heavy pilings out in advance of the vessel. Once the pilings were tamped down, block and tackle was employed to haul the boat forward to them. Then the pilings were pulled up, swung out and set down again. The procedure was repeated time and time again, inching the steamer along, and was used most often to get across dry sandbars. Another method was used when the sandbar was not "dry"; Captain Gill would turn the sternwheeler about and put her in reverse, then the paddle wheel would chew a channel right through the bar.

Several years had passed since Torn's last visit to North Fork Town, and he asked the bearded riverman about the place.

"You won't hardly recognize her," promised Captain Gill. "They put the Missouri, Kansas and Texas Railroad through there couple years back. And you still got the trail herds coming up the Texas Road. What's more, the emigrants are starting to use the ol' California Trail again to take 'em west through the Nations. You know the California Trail and the Texas Road cross at North Fork Town. Used to be a nice, quiet, little Indian village. But she's a wide-open, hellzapoppin' settlement these days."

The fourth day out of Fort Smith, Torn had an opportunity to see this for himself.

North Fork Town was and had always been the capital of the Creek Nation in Oklahoma. It had seen and survived its first boom in the days of the 'Forty-niners and the Colorado gold rush, when the California Trail had been, along with the Oregon and Santa Fe Trails, one of the main routes west across the frontier. During the war, following the Battle of Honey Springs, in which the Federals destroyed all organized Confederate resistance in the Nations, North Fork Town had been burned to the ground.

The Texas Road was responsible for the town's postwar resurgence. In the old days it had been a trace used by the Osage to carry their furs to St. Louis, before the arrival of the Civilized Tribes. When Texas cattlemen began to move their herds north to Kansas cowtowns, many used the old Osage route.

Now, too, the Missouri, Kansas and Texas Railroad—known as the KT or Katy—passed near North Fork Town. With railroaders, cowboys, emigrants and traders coming and going, the town thrived. Creeks came in from their farms to trade their produce for manufactured goods. The Creek schools and councils were held here. A brisk river trade kept the landing a mile northeast of town a busy place.

The *Jezebel* squeezed into a berth. The mooring lines were secured, the gangplanks run out. Torn took his leave as dockhands began unloading the steamboat's cargo. As he worked his way through the hustle and bustle on the landing, he spotted a handsome surrey with a team of matched bays in the traces, and a man he recognized sitting in the shade of the painted canvas top.

The man in the surrey saw Torn coming and stepped down to greet him with an outstretched hand.

"Clay, this is a surprise. Been a long time."

"Hello, judge."

Torn warmly shook J. Carter Ronan's hand, pleased to see the man who had saved his life ten years before.

CHAPTER 3

J. CARTER RONAN WAS A HEAVYSET MAN, WELL DRESSED in a blue broadcloth suit, with Middleton half-boots on his feet and a derby hat on his head. *He looks,* mused Torn, *as sleek and hardy as a mountain otter.* His walrus moustache and profuse side whiskers were neatly groomed. The late afternoon sun flashed off the solid gold watch chain arching across the front of his vest and the diamond stickpin in his silk cravat. Ronan smelled of French Quinine and money.

"A judge no longer, Clay," he chuckled. "I've hung up my robes, you might say."

"I heard you'd stepped down."

"No need to walk around the truth. They said I was corrupt. Threw me out."

Torn nodded. He'd met this man right after the war, when Ronan had been the judge at Fort Smith. Torn had been on the trail of Yankee deserters believed to be the abductors of his fiancée, Melony Hancock—a trail which had led him into the outlaw-infested Nations.

Back then, Torn had been a wanted man himself—wanted for the murder of Karl Schmidt, a sergeant of the guard at Point Lookout Prison. It was Schmidt's saber—or what was left of it—that Torn carried in the shoulder rig under his coat. He'd killed Schmidt during his escape from Point Lookout. As a result, the Federals had put a price on his head.

Finding his ancestral home in South Carolina destroyed, Torn had headed west in the closing days of the Civil War, bent on locating his fiancée. He didn't find Melony in the Nations, but he had played hell with the longriders who used the Indian Territory as a base of operations. He ended so many notorious careers—self-defense, in every case—that Judge Ronan had pulled some strings and obtained a full pardon for him.

Two years later Torn had been appointed a federal circuit judge—one of many gestures made by President Andrew Johnson intended to heal the wounds of civil war, a policy of appeasement which had eventually led to Johnson's impeachment. Prior to the war, Torn had studied law at the University of Virginia, a formal education that made him more qualified than many other frontier judges or justices of the peace.

"They were trumped up charges, Clay," insisted Ronan, striving to mask his bitterness. "I only sought to see the law applied fairly to one and all, but I came to realize that during the Grant years, judges in the South were not supposed to be fair and impartial. They were supposed to rubber stamp every oppressive action taken by the Occupation to grind the South under the heel of Reconstruction. I wouldn't play their game, so they got rid of me. I am eternally grateful."

"Why?"

"I'm making money hand over fist these days, Clay, I'm in business for myself. The Osage Trading Company, that's me. I freight manufactured goods into the Nations and take cotton and whatever else the Tribes produce back out. A lucrative enterprise."

"Sounds like it."

"Enough about me. What brings you to North Fork Town? Tell me, did you ever find . . . I'm sorry, but I can't recall her name."

"Melony Hancock." Torn shook his head, his voice and features bleak. "Not yet."

"My condolences."

Quick to change the subject, Torn said, "Big Mike Walker sent me a wire. It sounded like he was in some kind of trouble. Any idea what kind?"

"I can't help you, Clay." Ronan fished a stemwinder out of his vest pocket and consulted it. "I must see to a cargo that has just arrived. We'll talk later. Perhaps over dinner."

Torn agreed and moved on, bending his steps down the Texas Road. North Fork Town was a mile from the river, and the road, a wide stretch of rutted dust, was clogged with riders and wagons coming and going. He stuck to the edge of the road, trying to avoid the traffic and the dust.

He hadn't gone far when a wagon slowed beside him. The driver offered him a ride. Torn gratefully accepted.

"Windy Smith's my handle," said the driver, a wiry, sun-whacked character with a scraggly beard and squinty eyes beneath the pulled-low brim of a Kossuth hat. He yee-hawed the team into motion. "Called Windy 'cause I can spin a yarn a mile wide. Drive for a freight company these days, but I done ever' thing that's worth doin' in my time. Yessir, I have seen the elephant, and I have tales to tell. Used to scout for the Army against the Apaches—Cochise and his bunch. Let me tell you about Cochise, pilgrim. He was one mean red devil, I swear. He's the one shot an arrow in my leg. Still got a piece of the arrowhead stuck in the bone. It's the reason I hitch along like a three-legged dog. You see, we was hot on the trail of them broncos, deep in the Dragoon Mountains, and . . ."

By the time they reached town, Torn had concluded that Windy Smith could talk circles around Captain Gill.

The Texas Road narrowed as it entered the settlement. Scanning the buildings on both sides, Torn remembered what Captain Gill had said about recognizing the place. The *Jezebel*'s skipper had been right. Most of the log and clapboard structures now lining the town's main thoroughfare had not existed when he had last passed through here.

One building he did recognize was the jailhouse, built of yellow limestone. He asked Windy Smith to drop him off there. The talkative freighter obliged him, and as the wagon pulled away, Torn stepped into the jail.

It was empty. Returning to the boardwalk, he touched the brim of his hat to a pair of ladies passing by and looked up and down the Texas Road. The town was as busy as a beehive. He didn't see Big Mike Walker. Directly across the street was a long building of clay-chinked pine logs. A sign out front, decorated with fleurs-de-lis, indicated that this was Pete Shagrue's French Lily. Curious, Torn crossed the street. Opening one of a pair of doors set with ovals of etched glass, he stepped over the threshold and found himself shoved violently backward. He caught the heel of his boot and sprawled in the dust of the street.

Stunned, he looked up to find a black man standing on the boardwalk—one of the biggest men Torn had ever seen. Muscles threatened to rip the seams of the man's white muslin shirt. Bulging thighs stretched black twill trousers tucked into mule-ear boots. The man's fists were as big as sixteen-pound cannonballs. He flashed an amiable grin as Torn got to his feet.

"No hard feelin's, suh, but this here's a gennelmen's club, and you ain't no member."

Torn dropped his valise, laid his Winchester rifle across it, and brushed himself off.

"You could have just said so."

"Them's the rules."

"I have a rule of my own," said Torn, smiling faintly, "I go where I want, when I please."

He went in swinging.

CHAPTER

4

THE BLACK MAN WAS ASTONISHINGLY QUICK FOR ONE so big. Batting aside Torn's haymaker, he planted his fist in Torn's midsection. The blow lifted Torn clean off his feet. He hit the hardpack sucking air. Sheer will and stubborn pride got him back on his feet. He couldn't seem to straighten up. The black man was still standing on the boardwalk, watching him with open admiration.

"You's one tough customer," he said.

"Thanks for the compliment," wheezed Torn, and feinted a gut punch with his right. The black man dropped his guard, and Torn's left struck like a rattler, a solid cross to the chin. The black man rocked slightly on his heels. His backhanded swipe drove Torn into one of the boardwalk posts. Wood splintered. Torn careened off the post and fell on his face. Rolling away, he fetched up against the wall of the French Lily.

The black man rubbed his jaw. A trickle of scarlet leaked

out of the corner of his mouth. He looked at the blood on his fingers, then at Torn. He was still grinning.

"That's one mean left, suh."

As the black man lumbered forward, Torn entertained a fleeting and unsportsmanlike notion concerning the saber-knife under his coat. This man was without question the biggest, strongest character he had ever come across. He could kill with his bare hands. He could break bones as though they were dry twigs. He could tear a man apart limb from limb. Torn thought his only chance was to use a weapon. But in the end, he just couldn't bring himself to pull the saber-knife. An accomplished knife fighter, he could disable without killing, but he had never used blade or gun on an unarmed man, and he wasn't about to start now.

Torn got up, his back to the wall, keeping his arms down. As he hoped, the black man hurled a fist at his head. Torn ducked, and the fist bounced off one of the logs in the wall. The black man grunted in pain. Torn hammered him in the guts. It was like hitting a slab of rock. The black man drove an elbow into Torn's face. Torn struck the wall of the French Lily and slid down to the boardwalk.

"You stay down, you hear?" growled the black man.

Spitting blood, Torn started to get up. He moved slowly, clumsily, like he was at the end of his rope. The black man shook his head and moved in to finish him off, waiting for Torn to stand, too fair a fighter to hit him when he was down. This was what Torn was counting on. He drove a fist up between the black man's legs. The black man reeled away, knock-kneed. His blood up, Torn pounced on his adversary and slammed him into the wall. The black man staggered, stunned and wheezing. Torn channeled every ounce of strength he had left and hurled the goliath off the boardwalk. Landing on the cross rail of a hitching post, the black man somersaulted, landed on the back of his neck, and was out like a light.

Two men emerged from the French Lily. One, wearing a barkeep's canvas apron, rushed to the black man and pressed the side of his neck with two fingers, feeling for a pulse.

"Is he alive?" asked Torn, swaying on uncertain legs.

"Yes." Awestruck, the man in the apron gave Torn a long look, top to bottom. "I never thought I'd see the day when Hoke here got his plow cleaned."

"That was a dirty trick," remarked the other man, with a slow Southern drawl that was scarcely more than a whisper. "And I thought you were a gentleman, Judge Torn."

"I don't know you," said Torn.

"No, we've never met, but I know about you. A tall man in black, who carries a honed-down saber under his coat."

"You have sharp eyes."

"Weapons are a hobby of mine. That one has the look of a Chicopee saber. Made by a metalsmith named Ames up in Chicopee, Massachusetts, I believe."

Torn was surprised. "As a matter of fact, you're right."

"Jack," called the apron wearer, "help me get Hoke out of the street."

"A minute, Bill." Wearing a lazy smile, the man stuck out his hand. "Permit me to introduce myself. Jack Capehart's the name. They call me Whispering Jack."

Torn nodded and shook the hand. The name rang a bell. "I've heard of you."

Whispering Jack Capehart was, among other things, a lawyer. Those other things included gunslinger and gambler. It was said of Whispering Jack that he rarely lost a client and never lost at cards. He was the outlaw's best friend before the bar.

That whispery drawl was his trademark. Capehart could

mesmerize juries with the supple skill of a snake-charmer; his courtroom theatrics were legendary. So were his gun duels. Like another frontier legend, Wild Bill Hickok, Whispering Jack walked that fine line separating the lawless from the law-abiding.

"Lend a hand, Jack," persisted the barkeep.

Capehart stepped out into the slanting heat of the afternoon and helped transfer the unconscious Hoke into boardwalk shade. Torn helped, too. He laid Hoke's head down gently on the planking.

"I hated to do it," admitted Torn. "But he could have killed me without half trying."

"He killed a man once with his bare hands," said Capehart. "Back when he was a prizefighter. It was an accident, but accidental or not, dead is still dead."

"Hoke's a good man," defended the bartender. "Strong as an ox and a real skull-buster, but he's got a gentle heart. Don't worry, mister, he won't hold a grudge."

"I'm glad to hear it."

"I never thought I'd meet a man who could put Hoke down for the count," said Capehart.

"I didn't fight fair," said Torn.

"Well, I just hope we never get crossways with one another, Judge, because I don't, either."

CHAPTER 5

WHISPERING JACK CAPEHART WAS A SHARP DRESSER. He wore a blue frock coat, gold vest, nankeen trousers, and hand-tooled boots polished to a high sheen. Beneath a flat-brimmed planter's hat, his hair was shoulder length, the color of rust on iron. His face was sharp-featured, clean-shaven. A wide, red cummerbund encircled his slim waist. Carried butt forward in the sash was a .44 Dance revolver with terra cotta grips, and a Bowie knife with a staghorn handle.

"What happened, anyway?" he asked.

"I wanted to go inside," said Torn. "He didn't want me to."

"Just doing his job. Hoke is Pete Shagrue's bouncer. You see, Pete sells liquor, but he can't sell it to just anybody. It's against the law to sell to the Indians, so Pete runs a members-only club. That's part of the agreement he's hashed out with the Creek authorities. You can't be a member if you've got a drop of Indian blood in your veins."

"It's a mighty dumb law, you ask me," threw in the bartender. "Must be a dozen bootleggers doing a brisk business on the outskirts of town right this very minute."

"Law is law," replied Whispering Jack. "Some are of the opinion that laws are made to be broken, but not by Pete Shagrue. Not that one, anyway. If he does, the Creeks might throw him out of the territory."

"You're saying I have to be a member to get a drink?" asked Torn.

"That's the long and short of it," nodded the barkeep.

"How much does a membership cost?"

"A hundred dollars."

"I'm sorry I asked."

"Keeps out the cowboys," said Whispering Jack.

"And federal judges."

"Only the honest ones," smiled Capehart. "You can be my guest. Come on inside."

"What about Hoke?" asked the barkeep.

"Let him sleep it off. He'll be as good as new when he comes to."

Inside, Torn took one look around and decided a saloon by any other name was still a saloon. The mahogany bar stretched down the right side and two rows of deal tables covered with green felt stretched down the left. A couple of men in suits sat a table near the back. They threw curious glances at Torn and Capehart, wondering what the commotion had been about, then returned to their conversation. The apron went around behind the bar while Torn and Whispering Jack bellied up to it.

"What's your pleasure?"

"Bourbon, if you've got it."

"We do—bonded."

"No rotgut sold here," grinned Capehart. "Pete ships in the best labels, which is one of the reasons he had to hire Hoke. When an Indian gets tired of white lightning and decides he wants a real drink, he's sometimes hard to stop. But Hoke gets the job done. And then you have the occasional trailhand who thinks he's tough as rawhide. They find out real quick what tough is when they tangle with Hoke."

The bartender set a shotglass filled to the rim with amber liquor in front of Torn. Taking a sip, Torn swished it around in his mouth to wash away the coppery aftertaste of blood, then knocked back the rest of the shot.

"How is it?" asked Capehart.

"Damn fine coffin varnish."

Capehart motioned for the barkeep to refill Torn's glass.

"Ran into an old friend of yours down at the landing," said Torn. "Judge Ronan."

Capehart smirked. "Old friend, you say? Not hardly. He tried to hang them, I tried to save them."

"Some of the men you saved from the noose weren't worth saving."

"Every man is entitled to the best defense money can buy."

"Stolen money, in most cases."

"Allegedly stolen money," corrected Capehart. "But the old hanging judge and I don't dabble in law much any more. He's making money trading with the Indians and I'm making money playing poker and racing my Kentucky pure-blood."

"How are the pickings?"

"You wouldn't believe."

"Know Big Mike Walker?"

"Sure I do."

"Know where I can find him?"

Whispering Jack took a claro cigar out of a coat pocket,

bit off one end, and lit the other with a china match.

"Can't say that I do. Why do you ask?"

"Just curious." Torn deemed it unwise to confide in Whispering Jack; he didn't know Capehart well enough. And he didn't rule out the possibility that Capehart was part and parcel of the problem about which Big Mike had written him. Whispering Jack's reputation was shady. Torn finished off the bourbon and thanked Capehart.

"My pleasure, Judge."

Stepping out onto the boardwalk, Torn saw that Hoke was still out cold. He realized it had been his own pride that had triggered the altercation. Hoke had just been doing a job. But the war and his years on the frontier had given Torn a hard, violent edge. And pride had seen him through his sixteen months of living hell at Point Lookout Prison. He'd learned that when a man got knocked down he had to come up fighting, and it was a habit too hard to break.

Still, he felt a twinge of remorse. He hadn't fought fair. In his younger years, before the war, in a time that now seemed remote and dream-like, he'd been brought up to believe that gentlemen settled their differences in accordance with a strict code of honor. The war had shown him— and countless others—the folly of that way of thinking. A person did what was necessary to stay alive, and Clay Torn was nothing if not a survivor.

The day was coming to a close. The sun had set behind wooded bluffs west of town, and it's dying light touched the broad strokes of mare's tail clouds with lavender and old rose. A trio of Texas cowboys—wiry young men with sun-dark faces and dusty range clothes—were driving a hundred head of lanky longhorns north up the Texas Road. Torn waited until they had passed, then crossed to the jail in the settling dust.

He figured that waiting at the jailhouse was the best

way to meet up with Big Mike Walker. Dumping his valise and rifle inside the door, he settled down in the chair behind Walker's desk, propped his feet up, and was dozing before long.

When he snapped awake it was slap dark. He heard voices outside, and something in those voices alarmed him. A horse whickered. Someone pounded down the boardwalk at a run. Lighting a coal oil lamp, Torn went to the door and stepped out into a quickly gathering crowd.

"What's going on here?" he asked.

They were clustered around a horse, and one man had hold of the bridle while two more gingerly drew the body draped across the saddle to the ground. Torn pushed through a circle of grim-faced men and knelt beside the body. The lamplight played across the ashen features of Big Mike Walker.

"Is he dead?" someone asked.

Torn searched for and failed to find a pulse. He rolled Big Mike over and saw the bulletholes and a big, black stain of blood on Walker's shirt.

"Yes," he said flatly. "He's dead. Backshot."

TORN SENT ONE MAN FOR THE DOCTOR. ANOTHER helped him carry Big Mike Walker's body into the jailhouse where they laid him out on the desk.

"Someone should tell Long Walker," said the man assisting Torn, a young Creek half-blood in store-bought clothes.

Torn nodded grimly.

Long Walker was one of the tribal elders. Torn had met him once before, and remembered Long as a wise, compassionate man, highly respected by his people. He was Big Mike's father.

"Will you?" asked Torn.

The solemn young man thought it over. "I would rather cut out my tongue than carry such news to Long Walker. His heart will bleed."

"I'll do it, then."

The Creek had serious reservations about that.

"No, I will go. It would not do for him to hear it from a stranger."

Torn didn't waste breath telling him that he and Long were not complete strangers. It had been a long time; it was possible Long had forgotten him. Besides, it was not the kind of errand Torn cared for.

The man who had grudgingly accepted the role of messenger of death had not been gone long when North Fork Town's doctor arrived. An older man with skin like creased leather and gimlet eyes beneath a scowling brow, his first act was to clear the room. Everyone but Torn quickly filed out into the night.

"I said everybody," rasped the sawbones. "That means you too, mister."

"Reckon I'll stay."

Something in Torn's faint smile, and in the calm way the declaration was made, convinced the doctor that argument was useless. Laying his black grip on the desk beside Big Mike's body, he opened it and extracted a pair of wire-rimmed spectacles. Hooking the see-betters over his ears, he gave the corpse a cursory once-over.

"Been dead a few hours. What happened?"

"He was shot in the back."

"Help me turn him over."

Torn did so.

"Looks like .50 caliber or better to me," said the sawbones after a quick glance.

"You can tell just by looking at the holes in his clothes?"

The doctor peeled off his spectacles and gave Torn a withering look.

"I've been practicing in the Nations for twenty-odd years, so I've seen a few gunshot wounds."

"His holster's empty," remarked Torn.

"I'm not blind."

"Just ornery."

The doctor glowered, blinked, and sighed. He pinched the bridge of his nose with thumb and forefinger.

"Sorry. I liked Big Mike. It makes me somewhat hostile when I see a man I liked get killed. Name's Crane. What's yours?"

"Torn."

"You're a federal judge, aren't you?"

Torn said that was so.

"What are you doing here?"

"Big Mike sent me a wire. Said he needed help." Torn's tone grew bitter. "I got here a little too late."

"Wonder who did this and why?" muttered Doc Crane.

"I was hoping you'd have some ideas."

Crane snorted. "Wearing a badge in these parts buys you a lot of enemies."

"Damn," muttered Torn, frustrated. He had a sinking feeling that the only man who could have told him why Big Mike had sent the wire was Walker himself. Big Mike had been too close-mouthed for his own good, and now his lips were sealed forever.

"Somebody better go fetch Long," breathed Crane.

"It's been seen to."

"Good, good. Long lives at the edge of town these days, so he'll be here in a minute. We'd best turn Mike over on his back."

Torn agreed. It would be better if Long did not see the blood and bulletholes.

Soon thereafter, Long Walker appeared. Eighty winters old, Long was tall, thin, as bent and tough as a high country cedar sculptured by a relentless wind. Beleaguered by rheumatism, he relied on a hickory cane. His white hair brushed bony shoulders and his skin was like old parchment, so thin Torn could see bone. Despite the sultry warmth of the evening, he wore an old blanket coat and overalls. He looked like the hardscrabble farmer he was; nothing in his appearance suggested his power in the Creek Nation. A member of the tribal council, his word was heeded by all the Creeks.

Seeing Big Mike sprawled dead on the desk gave him pause as he entered the jailhouse. Torn saw him tremble, slump, then stiffen. His chin rose a fraction. His dark eyes bright, he made his way across the room and gazed for a full minute at Mike's face. The minute seemed to Torn like an hour.

Finally Long turned to peer at Torn, and Torn could see that the old Creek remembered him. The mind was still keen, and when he spoke the voice was still strong.

"How do you read this?"

"It was done out in the brush," guessed Torn. "His horse has traveled far today. Whoever killed him put him across the saddle and let the horse go, knowing it would bring the body back home."

"I see no wounds."

"He was shot in the back; ambush. He was too much to take on face to face. They didn't have the guts to give him a fair chance."

"He sent for you."

"Yes," said Torn, encouraged. "He told you that? Did he tell you why?"

Long's slow headshake dashed Torn's hopes.

"I could see he was troubled. But when I asked he would not tell me. He said he did not want to worry me. Of course, then I worried more. He spoke highly of you. You he would have told."

"But I didn't get here in time."

"Don't blame yourself."

"I do, though. And I promise you this: I'll get the man

or men who killed your son. Today they signed their own death warrants."

Long Walker gently removed the ball-pointed star from Big Mike's shirt and held it out to Torn.

"I will give you this and you will be Creek law."

"But I'm not Creek..."

"No matter. I wish it. The people will agree to it. I will speak to the council. I will say to them that you are the one my son sent for. That though you are white, you respect our ways."

Torn hesitated. "I don't know, Long."

"You have no power here unless we give it to you. Besides, who else could take my son's place?"

"The lighthorse..."

"They are all many days ride from here. The Kiowas and Comanches are raiding isolated farms and villages to the west. The lighthorse are all out there trying to stop them. It takes time to choose a Creek lawman. The tribe must be summoned, and days will pass to give those who wish to, time to come. And then two or three men picked by the council will be told to walk in different directions. The man who is followed by the most people when he walks away is chosen. This is our way."

"Sounds like a good way."

"But it takes time. A warm trail is easier to follow. I will tell the council this. And I will tell them that since a white man killed my son, it is better that a white man hunt down the killer."

Torn was quick to follow Long's reasoning. "Yes, I'm afraid you must be right. Backshooting is the way of some white men. A Creek would have too much honor."

"Then you accept."

Torn took Big Mike's badge and slipped it into his coat pocket.

CHAPTER

7

A WEEK LATER, TORN WAS PREPARING TO MAKE HIS
evening rounds; he was taking the sawed-off Fox shotgun
from the jailhouse gun rack when Angevine showed up.

Her coming was not a complete surprise. He had been
expecting it. Dreading it, in a way.

She stood a moment just inside the door, unsure of
herself and of the situation. He was beguiled by her beauty,
just as he had been years before. The passage of time had
had no effect on her.

The product of a French father and Creek mother, Angevine was tall and willowy, her flawless skin like copper
with honey highlights, her hair cherry-colored. Her hazel
eyes were big, bright, and bold. She wore a simple brown
skirt and white blouse, a wide leather belt around her
slender waist, and moccasins on her tiny feet.

"You haven't changed a bit," he said.

"I didn't know if I should come," she replied. "I heard

you were here. I kept telling myself he knows where I live; he can find me if he wants to. I waited and waited. It's been the longest week of my life. I finally decided you just didn't want to see me again. Or that you had forgotten."

"I haven't forgotten," he said woodenly.

Her lips thinned and her hands balled up into fists. She was cross, he could tell. Strong emotions were on a mad rampage beneath that mask of impassivity all Indian women are asked to master.

"I figured by this time you'd be married," he added. "Or moved."

"Where would I go? This is my home. My family is buried here. My friends are here."

"I can't believe some young man hasn't taken your heart, Angevine."

"It's already taken."

"Angevine . . ." he groaned.

"The young men seldom come courting any more," she said with a quirky smile. "They're beginning to say I'm a witch or something, living alone in a cabin in the woods. I guess you haven't found her, have you?"

"No."

"But you're still looking."

"Still."

She drew a long breath. "You're not wearing the badge."

"I've got it with me."

"My heart cries for Long Walker. Why was Big Mike killed?"

"I wish I knew. No one seems to have a clue."

"What will you do?"

"Poke around; keep my eyes open. It's the only thing I *can* do."

"That might take some time."

He went to the window and looked out at the night, acting like he was keenly interested in any activity that might be taking place on the Texas Road, while in fact all he hoped to do was avoid looking at her. It hurt him every time he laid eyes on her. It made him doubt himself; question his obsession with finding Melony Hancock.

"A friend, Mary Paige, is getting married tomorrow night," she said in a small, wistful voice. "People will come from all over. There will be food and dancing. They talked of postponing it, because of what happened to Big Mike, and out of respect for Long, but Long would not hear of it. I must be there."

Torn knew what she was getting at, and he was too much the gentleman to make her put it into words. He wanted to decline, but he couldn't bring himself to hurt her, even when failure to do so would mean plenty of hurt for himself.

"I'd be honored," he said.

She stood there, a ghost of a smile playing with her lips, and he knew she was hoping for more. Aggravated at himself for being so susceptible, Torn took his hat off a wall peg, planted it on his head, and shoulder-racked the scattergun.

"I think I'll take a look around."

She went out and he followed at a safe distance, standing on the boardwalk while she climbed into a rickety buckboard. He knew he ought to go through the motions of helping her aboard, but he didn't care to get that close. She was too much of a temptation.

"Tomorrow, then," she said, and whipped up the old plow mare in the shafts.

Torn watched her until she turned off the Texas Road, at the intersection that marked the center of North Fork Town, heading west on the California Trail. Trying to steer his thoughts away from her, he looked north and south, scanning the length of the Texas Road. A dog barked off in the distance. A hot, dry wind whispered in the alleys. He crossed to the other side, the moonlight throwing his shadow long across the rutted hardpack.

For a week now he had prowled the streets of North Fork Town, mostly at night, hoping sheer luck would bring him face to face with a clue to the mystery of Big Mike's murder. Nobody seemed to know anything. Maybe someone knew and just wasn't talking. Torn was determined to find out, if he had to stay until hell froze over.

Tonight, as in past nights, all was quiet. He bent his steps north, passing closed shops, Hungate's General Store, The Drover's Restaurant, a barber shop. North Fork Town resembled many other frontier settlements, with one glaring exception—no saloons. If the cowboys and railroaders wanted strong-water, they had to go into the woods and get it from bootleggers, or try their luck with Hoke at the French Lily.

Torn slipped into an alley between a bootmaker's shop and The Keystone Hotel. He had learned that most of these concerns were owned and operated by white men. The law of the Creek Nation prohibited anyone from residing or doing business in the Nations unless that person was married into the tribe, or was Creek himself. Most white businessmen, J. Carter Ronan included, had taken Indian wives in order to qualify. *Anything for a fast buck*, mused Torn.

And there was plenty of money to be made here, with the railroad, cattle herds, and emigrant wagon trains.

The subject of Indian women turned his thoughts back to Angevine. They'd met during his previous visit. Her brother had been a horse trader killed by outlaws, the same gang of desperadoes Torn had been tracking at the time. He'd been the bearer of this bad news to Angevine, who had recently lost her parents. It was this, realized Torn, that they had in common, for at the time he had been trying to come to terms with the death of his own folks and the disappearance of his fiancée. They'd given each other strength and comfort.

He could look back now and see that his relationship with Angevine had been a turning point in his life. He'd been forced to choose between a fairly normal, peaceful life with her, or the life he now led—a grim, rootless life of violence, loneliness, and searching.

Seeing Angevine again made him wonder whether he had made the wrong choice. Even more disturbing was the fact that he was going to be given another chance to make the same decision all over again.

The alley emptied into a vacant lot where windblown trash was impaled on waist-high clumps of beavertail cactus. He inadvertently kicked an empty glass bottle, which spun away to clank against a rusted wheel rim. He turned north, a silent shadow in a world of shadows, passing behind the log and clapboard structures lining the east side of the Texas Road.

Reaching the back corner of the French Lily, he stopped suddenly, his breath catching in his throat. From the alley came a furtive rustling sound. He peered into the darkness and thought he saw a shadow move. Catlike, he slipped into the alley, shotgun ready.

He found a door in the north side of the French Lily, tried the latch, and found it locked from the inside. He checked a pile of empty crates. Nothing. Moving on to the juncture of the alley with the Texas Road, he saw no one. He took a few steps out into the road and turned back to scan the front of the gentleman's club. The doors with their ovals of etched glass were closed. He could see the

mahogany bar with its brass footrail through a plate glass
window. The barkeep was polishing shotglasses with his
apron and stacking them in a pyramid on top of the bar.

Torn sidestepped so that he could see the length of the
French Lily. Several men sat at a table in the very back.
He had learned that this was Whispering Jack Capehart's
table, and most nights Capehart could be found here, thin-
ning the bankrolls of other "gentlemen."

Tonight, Whispering Jack was conspicuous by his absence. The chair reserved for the flamboyant, gun-toting
lawyer—the one in which he sat to put his back to the
wall—was empty. Torn moved closer to the window. He
could see the pile of chips and bottle of sour mash at the
empty chair. Evidently Capehart had stepped away for a
moment. Torn identified two of the three men present.
One was Boone Sowerwine, the owner of the Keystone
Hotel. Another was John Moultrie, a cattle buyer. Torn
didn't see Hoke, and wondered if the bouncer was fully
recovered from their altercation of a week ago.

Moving on, he reached the California Trail and turned
east, heading for Broken Wagon Road. There, on the edge
of town, near the tracks of the Katy Railroad, stood a
dismal row of shacks where prostitutes lived and worked.
Some lively wit, tongue firmly planted in cheek, had named
it Virgin Alley.

Torn had been surprised to find that the Creeks toler-
ated the presence of sporting ladies. Long Walker had
explained that they did so to protect their own women.
The soiled doves of Virgin Alley kept rowdy trail hands
and hard-living railroaders occupied. Torn surmised that a
similar line of reasoning moved the Creeks to turn a blind
eye to the bootlegging trade. As long as the drinking and
whoring was confined to the outskirts of town, the Creeks
were satisfied.

For the most part, Torn had steered clear of Virgin Alley. He did not like to witness the squalid misery; he didn't care to look into the eyes of lost souls. And he did not deem it wise to observe the indiscretions of some of North Fork Town's respectable citizens.

Torn reached the tracks, looked up and down Broken Wagon, saw nothing out of the ordinary, and retraced his steps, the Fox scattergun resting in the cradle of his arm. Another quiet night. Torn shook his head, discouraged. He felt like a mouse in a maze, not knowing which way to turn. Big Mike had been in big trouble, and he couldn't find a trace of it anywhere. He wished something—anything—would happen.

And right then his wish came true.

A woman screamed bloody murder. . . .

CHAPTER

8

IT WAS THE KIND OF SCREAM THAT COULD RIP THE FAB-
ric of the night and slice right through to the bone. Torn
felt the blood in his veins run ice-cold. That was a scream
of unspeakable terror, not just fear. The scream of someone who saw death coming. It made his spine crawl.

Pulse racing, he broke into a run. As he reached the
intersection of Broken Wagon and the California Trail, he
saw movement out of the corner of his eye. A man was
running south across the California Trail, angling away from
Torn, toward the dark shadows in the alleys and vacant
lots behind the row of buildings facing the Texas Road.

"Hold it!" shouted Torn.

The man put on a burst of speed. Torn swung the
scattergun in that direction. Pure reflex; he knew the
range was too great for a short-barreled shotgun.
The Fox in his left hand, he reached for the Colt
Peacemaker at his side. He drew the gun partway, then

hesitated. The man vanished into the night.

Torn ran down the California Trail, knowing he could have dropped the man had he drawn and fired, knowing just as well he wouldn't have done it. He had no proof the running man had committed a crime, even though flight was very often a solid indication of guilt.

Then he heard a second scream. It came from Broken Wagon north of the California Trail—Virgin Alley.

He turned and ran for the sound.

Arriving back at the crossroads, he saw a woman stagger out into Broken Wagon. She stumbled and fell. As she crawled, clawing at the hardpack, she made short wheezing sounds.

He hurried to her, bent down. Her skin was like marble in the moonlight.

"Are you hurt?"

She turned her face toward him, and he saw sheer terror. She tried to speak, but couldn't push the words past the panting gasps. She moved her arm in a jerky, convulsive motion.

His instincts told him she hadn't been hurt—not physically, at least—but she was very badly frightened. As frightened as a person could get.

He took a quick look around. Other women were emerging from their shanties, timid as prairie dogs coming out of their holes.

"Get back inside!" he yelled.

They vanished.

Hearing footsteps, he stood and spun around, leveling the shotgun. The man stopped dead in his tracks.

Torn didn't recognize J. Carter Ronan at first. He had always been dressed to the nines, in fine broadcloth suits and silk cravats, as befits a man of his stature in the community, whenever Torn had seen him.

Tonight, Ronan was shirtless and barefoot. He had his trousers on, suspenders dangling, and that was about it. He carried his Middleton half-boots in one hand. The rest of his clothes were draped over an arm. He didn't look at all dignified. His small, sloped shoulders and bulging belly were matted with hair. His big, square face, framed by that bushy set of muttonchop whiskers, was darkly flushed. He was embarrassed, realized Torn. Embarrassed that he, a man of his position, had been discovered here in Virgin Alley.

"Judge Ronan," said Torn. He didn't know what else to say.

"Clay, I . . ." Ronan scowled, cleared his throat, and tried to inject a little authority into his tone of voice. "What is happening here?"

"I don't know," replied Torn, turning quickly away.

The woman on the ground was still gasping and gesturing. Torn looked to his right and saw that the door to one of the shacks stood ajar. A peculiar crimson light issued from within. His first thought was that a fire had started. These shanties, made of rawboard and shakes, were tinderboxes. The whole street could go up in a flash. But he saw no smoke, heard no flames.

He moved to the door. At the last second before crossing the threshold, he had an almost overpowering urge to turn away. He had a strong feeling he wasn't going to like what he would see inside. A cold shudder wracked him from hat to heels. He'd never run away from anything before, but he wanted to now, and the sensation dazed him. He steeled himself and stepped inside.

Judge Ronan was coming in behind him. Torn pulled up sharply, like a blind man who walks into a wall. For all his bulk, Ronan couldn't budge Torn. Then he took a look over Torn's broad shoulder, and stopped all forward motion.

He made a funny noise and pivoted. Torn listened to him stumble across the narrow board sidewalk connecting the shacks and heard him gagging.

Torn's stomach did a slow, nauseating roll. Breathing high and fast, he tasted bile and swallowed hard. He couldn't move. His feet were rooted to the floor.

He stood there and stared into hell.

The walls were smeared with blood; blood was everywhere. It was the reason for the peculiar reddish light. A kerosene lamp burned, reflecting off the scarlet walls, its glass chimney splattered with more blood.

There was something on the rumpled, blood-soaked sheets of the narrow, iron bed against the far wall. Something resembling raw meat, with dead eyes staring straight at him.

CHAPTER

9

WHEN JUDGE RONAN CAME TO CALL, TORN WAS SITTING behind the desk in North Fork Town's stone jailhouse, staring blankly at the opposite wall. He wasn't seeing the wall. He couldn't get the Virgin Alley slaughterhouse out of his mind. Ronan's entrance brought him back to the present.

Torn had been expecting this visit.

Ronan was fully dressed now, once again flush with eminence and composure. Casting a furtive glance at the pair of strap-iron cells in back, and noting with relief that they were empty, he approached the desk wearing a smile that was tight at the corners.

"Clay," he said, adopting a tone usually reserved for lifelong friends, "I have only a moment, so I will speak bluntly. I've a personal request to make of you."

Torn shifted in the chair, suddenly uncomfortable.

"Yes," he said. "I thought so."

Ronan frowned. Torn figured being one step ahead of Ronan was presumptuous on his part, but he was in no mood for the games gentlemen played.

"There will, of course, be an inquest," said Ronan. "Long Walker will preside. He has scheduled it for tomorrow afternoon."

Torn nodded. "I hope it will be less painful for him than the one he presided over a week ago."

"You refer to the inquest into the sheriff's death," said Ronan absently. He was too wrapped up in his own problems to be concerned with Long Walker's feelings. "These things must be seen to. It is Creek law. He must report to the tribal council. You will be sworn to testify to everything you witnessed tonight."

"Yes."

Ronan cleared his throat and leaned on the desk.

"Clay, I must ask you to omit any reference to me in your testimony."

"I see." Torn felt suddenly tired.

His response was not sufficiently committal to satisfy Ronan.

"It is not for myself personally that I make this request, you understand." Ronan drew himself up to his full height. "It is for my wife, her peace of mind. This would . . . disturb her greatly."

"I guess it would."

Anger darkened Ronan's features. "You owe me a favor, Clay."

"I wondered when we'd get around to that."

"It was I who interceded on your behalf. You have me to thank for your pardon. You were a wanted man, wanted for the murder of that prison guard. The entire Federal Army was looking for you. They would have caught you, eventually. You would have been hanged."

"It's true you pulled some strings and got my pardon, but that was your end of the deal. I did my part. I killed Seminole Simms and broke up his gang."

"Which demonstrated to me that you would serve the country better as a force for law and order on the frontier than as crowbait dangling from a noose."

"You know why I came into the Nations and tracked down Simms and his bunch—because I had reason to believe that one or more of the men who'd abducted Melony rode with Simms. I thought it possible I might even find Melony herself."

"But you didn't."

Torn drew a long, slow breath. "No."

"I am sorry for that. The fact remains, I am, I believe, due special consideration."

Brooding, Torn tipped the chair back on its hind legs and rocked slightly.

"Your wife is Creek," he said. "A very influential family."

"Yes, but I don't see . . ."

"Give it a rest," said Torn sharply. "You can't reside here or do business here without permission from the Creeks. They'd take a dim view of your cheating on your wife, one of their own."

Ronan's jaws worked; he was literally grinding his teeth. "You bastard . . ."

"I'm not the one caught with his pants down in Virgin Alley while his wife was sitting at home."

Ronan's attitude changed abruptly. The bluster and indignation melted away. Shoulders slumping, he collapsed into one of the chairs facing the desk, the picture of dejection.

"You don't understand," he moaned. "She's my wife, yes. But she hasn't . . . behaved like a wife for quite some time. She doesn't have anything to do with me . . ."

This revelation caught Torn completely by surprise. Ronan was baring his innermost secrets and it did not come easy. Torn sensed that this was not merely a ploy to win him over.

"I didn't see you tonight," said Torn.

The words were bitter on his tongue. Lying was not easy for him, but that was exactly what he would have to do tomorrow at the inquest. The decision was a difficult one. Two considerations swayed him. First, he *did* feel as though he owed J. Carter Ronan. Secondly, if he told the whole truth and nothing but the truth, Ronan would be ruined. And that would be a greater wrong than lying to Long Walker.

Ronan was immensely relieved. He had humbled himself before Torn and he could not look Torn square in the eye. He seemed engrossed in picking lint from the sleeve of his broadcloth coat.

"I don't know how to thank you, Clay."

"Forget it," said Torn curtly.

Stricken, Ronan stood and made for the door. There he paused and looked back.

"It was a terrible thing. Who could have committed such an unspeakably depraved act? What kind of man could have? . . ."

Torn shook his head. He saw the blood-smeared walls again. The dead, staring eyes, wide with surprise. It was an indelible mental image, and he was afraid it would never fade.

"I'll be forever in your debt, Clay."

"Let's just say we're even," sighed Torn.

CHAPTER 10

NEEDING A DRINK LIKE HE'D NEVER NEEDED ONE BE-
fore, Torn walked down the Texas Road to Shagrue's
French Lily. This time the black man guarding the door
flashed a smile at him.

"John Law, welcome."

"Glad there are no hard feelings."

He headed for the mahogany and ordered bourbon and
branch water. Whispering Jack sat at the table in back,
playing solitaire. Several gentlemen sat at another table;
Torn did not know them. They were talking business in
low tones. *A lot of white speculators are getting rich in the
Nations,* mused Torn as he took his drink to a vacant table.

Capehart put down his pasteboards and walked over.

"Mind if I join you?"

Torn kicked a chair out.

"You don't look well," observed Whispering Jack, settling his lanky frame across the table. "I don't wonder. I

heard what happened on Broken Wagon. Cigar?"

"No thanks."

Capehart fired up a claro. "Happened to be out on the street a little while ago; saw Ronan leave the jailhouse. Was it a bribe? Or just sweet talk?"

"What do you mean?"

"Don't try to pull the wool over these old eyes."

"He just wanted to know what had happened."

"Did he now. He doesn't remember?"

"And how would you know he was there?"

"A little bird told me. Let me guess. He doesn't want you to tell anybody. He thinks it's a well-kept secret. Which it is—by almost everyone."

"You'd like to see him squirm, wouldn't you?"

"We never did see eye to eye, back when he was the judge at Fort Smith. He was Old Testament, right down to the ground. Dispatched men to the gallows with all the righteousness of an avenging angel."

"While you did your best to save every defendant, no matter how heinous the crime, from the hangman's noose."

"Better a hundred guilty men go free than one innocent man be put to death."

"Her name was Katy O'Keefe. Did you know her?"

Whispering Jack tugged on his moustache, neatly trimmed and waxed, and long enough to reach the stubborn line of his jaw.

"I don't get down to Broken Wagon much."

"You *did* know her."

"Let's say I knew *of* her."

"Don't tell me you're trying for respectability at this late date."

Capehart's rakish features were a smiling mask. "This *is* a gentleman's club."

"Since when were gentlemen respectable?"

"Did you find anything in Katy O'Keefe's room?"

"No. Why so interested?"

"I might have to defend the man who did it. If you catch him."

"Oh, I'll catch him," said Torn fiercely. "And you would, wouldn't you?"

"What?"

"Defend the man who butchered that woman."

"Everyone deserves a day in court."

"He deserves to burn in hell," said Torn.

"Perhaps."

"There's no question."

"There is always a question, always a motive; a reason for the most senseless and savage crime."

"I saw a man running away."

"Did you recognize him?"

Watching Capehart's reaction with close interest, Torn said, "Too dark. Too far away. Come to think of it, I don't know why it was too dark. The night's clear. The moon's full. Maybe a soul so dark makes it's own shadow."

"That's awfully poetic."

"I almost fired at him. I should have. I'm sorry now that I didn't."

"You did the right thing," said Capehart. "He might not have been the killer. You might have shot an innocent man."

"He wasn't acting innocent."

Capehart gave Torn a long, speculative look, then stood, stretching like a cat.

"To hell with it. I think I'll turn in." He took a step and paused. "I suppose they'll be burying Katy O'Keefe tomorrow. Will you be there?"

The question caught Torn off guard. He hadn't given the matter much thought.

"Yes, I think I will be."

"Good. Good." Capehart drew a deep breath. "Say goodbye to her for me, will you?"

"Why not do it yourself?"

Whispering Jack peered at him through blue cigar smoke trickling from between his lips.

"Will you?"

"Sure."

Capehart walked away. He said good night to Bill, who was behind the bar polishing glasses, and stepped out into the night. Torn listened to his boot heels strike the boardwalk, then fade away. Finishing his bourbon, he got up and left the French Lily. The night was hot, still, and lifeless. He wiped a sheen of clammy sweat from his forehead. His shirt stuck to his back. He looked up and down the Texas Road. Jack Capehart had vanished.

At that moment Torn remembered standing near this very spot earlier that evening and glancing through the plate glass, just minutes before hearing Katy O'Keefe scream. He remembered seeing men at Jack Capehart's poker table . . .

But no Whispering Jack.

C H A P T E R

11

WHEN DOC CRANE FINISHED HIS POST MORTEM, KATY O'Keefe's remains were wrapped in the blood-stained sheets, then in an old canvas wagon tarp lashed together with hardtwist. The body was removed to the livery where the owner and forge-master, John Eagle, labored into the early hours of the morning to build a coffin.

It was a service the old leather-skinned Creek had provided North Fork Town for many a year. He could also carve headstones. This time he did no carving; no one asked him to. As meticulous in his bookkeeping as he was in his work, John Eagle would submit a bill to the town council for the cost of the coffin. He had a longstanding agreement with North Fork Town, which footed the bill for the coffins of departed souls who either did not have a family to pay the funeral costs, or whose personal effects did not include cash money.

The pearly light of dawn found Torn at Katy O'Keefe's

shanty on the Broken Wagon line. A worse way to start the day could scarcely be imagined, but Torn saw the unpleasant task through. When he had a job to do, he did it.

He hadn't given the shanty a thorough search the night before, and he chided himself for his failure to do so. The sight of Katy O'Keefe's butchered body had thrown him off. He'd seen plenty of blood and death in his lifetime, but none of it had prepared him for the sight he had seen last night.

The body was gone, but the blood remained. The walls, the floor, the seedy furnishings—everything was covered with blood. The thin mattress on the narrow, iron bed had soaked up a lot; the smears on the wall had dried. But in places on the floor the blood had puddled so thickly that it hadn't dried completely. Torn got some on his hands. It was cold and sticky between his fingers. *Only hours ago*, he mused, *this had pulsed hot and strong through a woman's veins*. An odd reflection, and it depressed him to think of it.

He bent down to pull a carpetbag from under the bed. Blood had soaked through the carpetbag, staining a pair of once-white satin gloves with mother-of-pearl buttons, the kind of gloves high-flown ladies wore, covering their arms to the elbow. The only other item in the bag was a small, wooden box. Its lid was intricately carved. Torn opened the box. Inside was a lock of braided red hair.

He sat back on his heels, holding the lock of hair, wondering what it had meant to Katy O'Keefe. Whose hair was it? Man, woman, child? Of course, he had no way of knowing and probably never would. The lock of hair and the expensive gloves had been Katy's prized possessions. Her lips were forever sealed.

Besides the bed, the room contained two other pieces

of furniture: a table with a small drawer and a wooden chair that didn't look sturdy enough to sustain the weight of a child. A skirt was draped over the back of the chair. A waist, chemise, and petticoat were scarlet-splashed bundles on the floor. Torn saw one kid-and-cloth shoe. The other was missing.

The table drawer contained two bottles of laudanum, one nearly empty, the other half full. This discovery didn't surprise him. Many women in Katy O'Keefe's line of work resorted to opium preparations or whiskey, even small doses of belladonna, to ease the pain of broken dreams and bitter lives.

Also in the drawer was a comb, a broken mirror, a garter, and a small change purse. The purse contained a few shell hairpins and a pair of cheap earrings of colored glass. Not a red cent. No doubt Katy had spent her earnings on the laudanum she hoped would diminish the pain and tame the nightmares. There was no law on the books against the use or sale of opium preparations. A prostitute dying of an overdose was an all too common occurrence. Much of the time the overdose was intentional.

Torn confiscated the gloves and the wooden box containing the lock of red hair; someone would steal the rest of Katy's meager belongings before the day was done. It was in his mind to place the items in the grave, as it seemed only fitting that they remain with the person to whom they had meant something special.

About to leave, he paused at the door and gazed with sick wonder at the scene. Why had this happened? Did it have any connection with the murder of Big Mike Walker? What had Katy O'Keefe done to deserve such a horrible end? No one deserved to die like that. So why? What kind of man could have committed such an atrocity?

A man, thought Torn, *like Karl Schmidt*.

The Point Lookout sergeant-of-the-guard had been a brutal, sadistic monster, a man who liked nothing better than causing pain. He had caused Torn plenty, so much that Torn had lived for the day when he could repay Schmidt. In a way, Schmidt had given him a reason to live—revenge. And when that day came—when for one brief moment Schmidt grew careless—Torn had run the Yankee sergeant through with his own saber and escaped that hellish Union prisoner-of-war camp.

Yes, thought Torn, *a man like Schmidt could do a thing like this.*

He'd crossed the paths of some bad characters since Schmidt, but none to equal the brutish Yankee sergeant when it came to sheer savagery. He hadn't really believed there could be another man so bloodthirsty on the face of the earth.

Now he realized he'd been wrong.

CHAPTER 12

JOHN EAGLE TRANSPORTED THE COFFIN TO THE HILLTOP cemetery of North Fork Town in the bed of a spring wagon. His two sons had dug the grave. They used ropes to lower the coffin into the deep, dusty hole they had recently excavated.

Torn had wrapped the gloves in a strip of muslin; now he knelt at the rim of the grave and dropped them on top of the coffin.

The carved wooden box containing the lock of hair was in a desk drawer back at the jailhouse. He had a hunch the hair might be a clue that could lead him to Katy O'Keefe's killer and he could not bring himself to part with it.

"Whispering Jack asked me to tell you so-long," he murmured.

Standing, he nodded at John Eagle's two sons. They began to fill the grave. No priest or preacher had come to say words over Katy O'Keefe, and Torn thought she at

59

least deserved a prayer, but try as he might he couldn't remember how to pray. He listened to the shovels biting deep into the piles of dirt and heard the thump and clatter of loose earth and small stones striking the coffin. A thrasher, perched on the low rock wall encircling the cemetery, sang a sweet song. Locusts buzzed in the sycamore trees.

John Eagle whipped his mules into motion and Torn watched him go. As the wagon moved away, he saw a woman standing at the cemetery gate, framed by the stone columns. She stepped aside as the wagon passed through. Eagle touched the brim of his slouch hat. Torn started toward her. She began to walk away, a carpetbag in hand.

"Wait!" he called. "I'd like to talk to you."

She stopped and watched him apprehensively as he came closer. He halted ten feet from her, giving her plenty of elbow room, as circumspect as he would be with a high-strung bronc.

"Don't run away," he said. "You came to pay your last respects. Don't let me stop you. I'm glad somebody came."

"You did."

Her basque and skirt were forest-green velvet, a little frayed at the hems, with yellowed lace at collar and cuffs. She wore black lace gloves with the fingers cut out. Her dark green hat was embellished with a thin, yellow, satin ribbon. The clothes had seen better days, but Torn figured she'd done the best job she could of dressing up.

Belatedly he recognized her—the woman in the street last night. The one so frightened she'd scarcely been able to breathe. Her skin was white as alabaster, with a translucent quality; he thought he could almost see the bones in her face and hands. Her hair was light brown, her eyes hazel. She wore no rouge. Dark shadows lurked beneath her eyes. *Ten years ago*, he mused, *she'd been very pretty.*

But her life was a hard one. It took a heavy toll. She'd lost her beauty, her youth, her dreams, and now, apparently, her friend.

"How well did you know her?" he asked, wondering if she would lie.

She looked beyond him at the grave, and her pale lips parted slightly.

"Was she a friend of yours?" asked Torn.

"I don't have any friends."

"But you knew her."

"Not very well. No one did. Katy didn't talk about herself. We all have pretty much the same story."

"But you came here today."

The corner of her mouth curled in a jaded smile.

"I didn't know you'd be here, or I might not have."

She looked past him again. John Eagle's sons were tamping down the earth with the flats of their shovels. Strong emotion stirred beneath the impassive mask she tried to maintain.

"I believe you would have," said Torn.

"You think you're awfully smart," she said, with a curious lack of feeling, so that he couldn't tell if she was being sarcastic or just making an ambivalent observation. "So you're the new sheriff."

"Not really. I'm a federal judge."

"Judge, sheriff." She shrugged. "I haven't seen you down on the line much."

"I've only been here about a week."

"Still. Big Mike didn't walk the line much, either. Said he knew we had to make living and that a badge was bad for business. I wish you'd been there last night."

"So do I."

She pushed a stray tendril of hair back behind an ear. Her hand trembled slightly.

"It was all my fault," she said.

"How is that?"

"I have the shack next to hers. We tried to look out for each other."

"Did you see anything?"

She shook her head. "Nothing." She squeezed her eyes shut. She looked much older with her eyes closed, as though the only life left in her lingered in her eyes. "I heard her scream. I can still hear it. I guess I always will."

"What did you do?"

"Nothing." The eyes opened, flashed defiance. "I couldn't move. I was scared. Her scream was . . . you'd understand if you'd heard it."

"I did. I understand."

"I finally got my nerve up and went to the door. I was about to open it when I heard someone running by. A man."

"You saw him?"

"No. I jumped away from the door. I was afraid."

"Then how did you know it was a man?"

"I just know. His boots fell heavy and loud on the boards."

Then what happened?"

"A minute later I found the courage to open the door. The man was gone. Disappeared. I saw a light coming from the open door to Katy's shack. I went in . . . I'm afraid I don't remember much after that. I remember hearing another scream. Then I realized it was me screaming."

"Which way was the man running?"

"Toward the California Trail."

South on Broken Wagon, thought Torn. *And I was running north, headed straight for him.*

Could it have been the man he had seen crossing the California Trail? He didn't think so. He'd seen that man almost immediately after hearing the scream. He couldn't have been running past this woman's door at that moment.

Torn frowned. It didn't add up, unless . . . unless there had been two men fleeing Virgin Alley at the same time last night. It seemed this woman had heard her man at the same time he'd seen his.

So what had become of the second man, the one thundering past her door right after Katy's scream? He must have been heading straight for Torn as Torn stood looking east down the California Trail at the first man. He had seen Torn and found a place to hide. That was the best explanation.

Something else bothered him. Only a minute, two at the outside, could have elapsed between his hearing the first scream and his reaching Katy O'Keefe's place. How was it possible that the murderer had done so much damage in such a short time, and still managed to make good his escape?

"You have good eyes," she said, wistfully.

"What?" He'd been lost in thought.

"Honest eyes. A person's eyes are the mirrors of the soul."

The image of Katy O'Keefe's staring eyes flashed across his mind.

"What's your name?"

"Nellie. Nellie Bond. Not that it matters. I'm leaving."

"Where are you going?"

She shrugged her indifference. "The next town. Mc-Alester, maybe."

She made it sound like it didn't matter and Torn realized that it probably didn't. To a woman like Nellie Bond, the towns were like the men. One was as good or bad as the next.

"Have any money?" he asked.

She bit back an angry retort. It was none of his business, and he expected to be told as much. Instead, she said, "No. Not really."

He gave her all the money in his pocket. A ten-dollar gold piece and two half dollars.

"What do I have to do for this?" she asked.

He smiled. "Nothing."

She took the money. Like most women in her line of work, Nellie had her priorities in order. Survival came before pride.

Torn searched for words of encouragement. He wanted to tell her to think better of herself, not to give up hope, or give up on life, but he decided such words would only humiliate her.

"One more question," he said. "Do you have any idea who might have done this to Katy? Any enemies?"

She searched his face for a full half-minute in a very keen, disconcerting way, before answering.

"I think it was a mistake," she said flatly.

"What do you mean, a mistake?"

"Catch him, mister. Do it quick. Before somebody else dies."

She turned her back on him and started following the dusty wagon tracks curling down the rocky hillside.

"What do you mean, a mistake?" he repeated.

She kept walking, toting the carpetbag.

"Good luck," said Torn.

She flashed a savvy smile over her shoulder and twitched her hips.

"Luck has nothing to do with it," she replied.

He watched her go down the hill.

I think it was a mistake.

The forge-master's sons trudged past him through the

cemetery gate, shouldering their shovels.

Torn followed them down, gripped by a sense of urgency.

Before somebody else dies.

CHAPTER

13

IT OCCURRED TO TORN THAT KATY O'KEEFE'S MUR-
derer must have been covered with the blood of his victim
as he fled the scene of the crime. Leaving Doc Crane's
office, he returned to Virgin Alley, hoping to find a trail
he could follow. He searched all around Katy's shack, and
in the alley behind the Broken Wagon shanties. Nothing.

He went next to the vacant lot behind the buildings on
the east side of the Texas Road—the lot into which the
man he had seen last night had disappeared. For a time
all he found was trash, broken bottles, and rusted cans.
He disturbed shrikes nesting in the beavertail cactus. Vicious, noisy birds, the shrikes impaled their prey, grass-
hoppers, lizards, and field mice, on the cactus thorns.

The ground was covered with footprints. Many people
cut through the lot; while Torn was searching, a man
emerged from the alley between the Keystone Hotel and
the bootmaker's shop. He gave Torn a curious glance,

then moved on in the direction of the railroad tracks.

Torn was about to give up when he found the piece of cloth. A cactus pad had recently broken off one of the waist-high clumps, and the torn fabric was stuck to its inch-long yellow spines. Pulling the material free, Torn examined it closely, rubbing it between thumb and forefinger.

He was pretty sure it was pilot cloth, an expensive fabric, dark blue in color, with a heavy weave. Capes, cloaks, and overcoats of this material could be had, if you wanted to pay the price.

Torn thought back to last night. He was willing to bet the man he'd seen had been wearing a long cloak or coat. And that in itself was odd, as the night had been quite warm.

The coat or cloak might have been worn to conceal bloodstains on the clothes underneath it.

But if the man he'd seen entering this vacant lot had been the murderer, what about the man Nellie Bond had heard running past her door just after Katy's dying scream?

Torn shook his head. He was convinced he had a clue in the fragment of pilot cloth, but he needed more—a lot more—to figure this one out.

He headed for the Texas Road through the alley adjacent to the French Lily, and he was so wrapped up in his thoughts that he collided with Doc Crane coming off the boardwalk. Torn apologized and learned that the old sawbones was on his way to the inquest.

"Have the post mortem findings right here," said Crane. "Want to see them, I suppose."

Torn glanced over three sheets of paper filled with indecipherable hen-scratchings. Correctly interpreting Torn's expression as one of consternation, Crane plucked the report from his fingers.

"Never mind. I can tell you what it says. Not likely to forget in this lifetime. Katy O'Keefe's throat was cut, from left to right, with a knife, very nearly detaching the head from the torso. The abdomen was slashed across and downward, also from left to right, from the bottom of the ribcage to the pelvic arch. This cut was made with great violence. The blade of the knife scraped the vertebrae and left a quarter-inch gash in the crest of the ilium."

"The what?"

"Hipbone. A second cut was made, lower and parallel to the first. The stomach, liver, uterus, and other internal organs were perforated." Crane sniffed and looked down the hooked blade of his nose at Torn. "Let me put it this way: the killer gutted the poor woman, then hacked and stabbed repeatedly into the open wounds."

Torn grimaced. "A butcher," he muttered.

"He cut the throat first," continued Crane. "The carotid artery was severed. This accounts for all the blood on the walls and was the immediate cause of death."

"You're saying she was dead when he cut her open."

"Dead or dying."

"Can you tell me anything about the knife?"

Crane shrugged. "I estimate the blade was one-and-a-half to two inches wide, at least twelve inches long. Single-edged, extremely sharp."

"Most men in the Nations carry a long knife. Bowie, Arkansas Toothpick, something." With a rueful smile, Torn held open his frock coat, allowing Crane to see the saber-knife in its shoulder harness. "Even me."

Crane nodded. "Yes, that knife of yours could definitely do the job."

"What bothers me is that if he just wanted to kill her, cutting the throat was enough."

"It would have sufficed."

Crane sounded cross, and Torn could only guess why the doctor was so out-of-sorts. Even this man—one whose profession brought him face to face with death on a regular basis—was deeply distressed by the murder of Katy O'Keefe. Not just the crime itself—that was bad enough— but by the cruel dimensions of the act. Sadistic butchery of the sort inflicted upon Katy O'Keefe would shake any civilized man to the core.

"This man is depraved," said Crane. "He wanted to bathe in her blood. It's hard to believe that such people exist."

"I've met at least one," said Torn.

"When?"

"In the war. A sergeant in the Federal army, a prison guard. He's dead now."

"There's been a lot of talk about you around town," said Crane. "By all accounts, you're a brave man, but I urge you to take extreme care. The man you're after is worse than all the gunhawks and outlaws in the Territory put together."

"Problem is, I've got two killings now," said Torn. "First Big Mike, and now Katy O'Keefe. There doesn't seem to be any connection, but I . . ."

Crane was peering over Torn's shoulder into the alley running alongside the French Lily, and didn't seem to be paying any attention whatsoever to what Torn was saying.

Then the doctor's eyes widened. His mouth gaped open to shout a warning. Torn didn't wait to hear it. He whirled, pushing Crane with his left hand, reaching for the Colt Peacemaker with his right.

Two men were stalking down the alley, side by side, pistols in hand. Torn realized they'd been trying to Indian-up on him, to get as close as possible and make their first shots count.

When they saw the game was up, they started shooting.

Torn heard hot lead shimmy in the air and slap into the hardpack. He fired and moved at the same time, feeling the breath of a bullet on his cheek—entirely too close for comfort. In the road behind him, one of the leaders in a covered wagon's four-hitch was hit and went down screaming, throwing the other three horses into a panic. A farmer and his young wife sat in the wagon box. The farmer pushed his bride back under the wagon canvas and crawled in after her, seeking cover.

Diving for the boardwalk in front of the French Lily, Torn rolled and came up with his back to the wall at the corner of the building. He thumbed the Colt's cylinder open, let the empties clatter on the warped planking beneath his feet, and plucked new loads out of his gunbelt.

Bullets were still flying out of the alley. The two men seemed to be shooting with reckless abandon. Torn saw with dismay that the Texas Road was full of people—the usual midday bustle. Folks were scampering for cover. Men were shouting, women were screaming. Most of them didn't know where the gunplay was coming from, and in their panic were running right into the line of fire. A rider lost control of his horse; the animal reared and threw the man. He got to his feet staggering. Torn yelled a warning, then cursed under his breath as a slug caught the man in the arm, knocking him down.

That really burned Torn's bacon. The lives of innocent bystanders were being put at risk, and this forced him out into the open. He was sure the two men had come gunning for him, so he stepped into the alley, bold as brass, blasting away with the Peacemaker.

The alley was filled with a fog of gray gunsmoke. Torn turned his body slightly into target stance, his gun arm extended at shoulder height. A slug plucked his coattails.

He didn't flinch. It was one ambusher's last shot. As his hammer fell on an empty chamber, every trace of color bled out of the man's face. Torn turned his attention to the second gunman. The Peacemaker barked twice. The second man jackknifed and dropped to his knees, clutching his abdomen. He looked up at Torn, stunned, tried to lift his pistol. Advancing with slow, measured steps, Torn aimed and fired once more. A blue hole appeared in the man's forehead. The impact hurled him backward. The pistol, flung by a dead hand, struck the wall of the French Lily and discharged. The bullet went harmlessly skyward.

The first man let go a strangled cry as Torn's Colt swung toward him. He gave up trying to reload and darted for the French Lily's side door. Torn hesitated, thinking the door would be locked, as it had been last night, thinking also that he wanted to take this one alive if at all possible.

He had a hunch someone had put these two onto him, and he wanted to know who that someone was.

To his surprise, the door wasn't locked. As the ambusher vanished inside, Torn broke into a run.

Inside, a gun spoke twice. The man who had just disappeared inside came flying back out. He landed at Torn's feet, spread-eagled on his back, the two bulletholes in his shirt front smoldering. His boot heels drummed the ground. Then death claimed him.

Torn looked up and saw Whispering Jack Capehart standing in the doorway, the .44 Dance still smoking, held down by his side.

"His gun was empty," said Torn.

"Was it?" murmured Capehart, indifferent. "I didn't think to ask."

Torn knelt at the dead man's side, went through his pockets. Capehart stepped down into the alley, snugging the Dance under his red cummerbund, and strolled across to take a look at the other corpse.

"Seen them before?" asked Torn.

"Can't say that I have."

Torn found five gold double eagles in the dead man's pants pockets. Seeing this, Capehart searched the other man and found five more. He whistled softly.

"If I had to hazard a guess, I'd say these boys were paid to kill you, Judge."

"They were overpaid."

Capehart nodded. "By the looks of their clothes, and the calluses on their hands, I'd say they were common laborers. Rivermen, maybe. Dockhands. Not professional guns, obviously."

Torn stood, went over to Capehart, and held out his hand, palm up.

"I'll take that money."

Capehart's smile was crooked. "I killed one of them, remember?"

"The one I wanted to take alive. The one who might have told me who hired him. The money."

He'd made up his mind to give some of the double eagles to the wounded bystander and the rest to the young couple whose horse had been killed in its traces, but he didn't bother telling Capehart this.

Whispering Jack shrugged and put the five twenty-dollar gold pieces in Torn's hand.

Turning away, Torn left the alley. The throng of on-lookers parted like the Red Sea, giving him plenty of room to pass through. They sensed that he was a marked man.

The same thought occurred to him, but he wasn't both-ered by it.

In fact, he took it as a good sign.

CHAPTER 14

THAT EVENING TORN BRUSHED OUT HIS CLOTHES, SPIT-shined his boots and went off to John Eagle's livery to hire a rig. This he drove to Angevine's cabin a few miles outside of North Fork Town.

He knew the way, having been there before, years ago. The cabin was as he remembered it, not far from the California Trail, beneath tall sycamores and overcup oaks, the trees a ragged rank of silent sentinels standing guard along the purling Canadian. His last visit had been to bring the news of her brother's death to Angevine. The memory stitched a grim frown on his face.

She looked particularly fetching tonight. She wore a white blouse and turquoise skirt. Her cherry-colored hair gleamed in the moonlight, draping her coppery shoulders, and her long bangs were a veil through which big hazel eyes bathed him in a warm light that was unsettling.

He drove the rig back to the Texas Road and turned

south. The council house was a few miles from town. Torn figured half the Creek Nation would be there. Not being much for shindigs, he was in no real hurry to arrive.

It was a sultry, summer night. Angevine sat close beside him, and her sweet woman-smell filled his senses. She was desirable and he desired her. He was a red-blooded male and there was no help for it, but he felt the shape of Melony's photograph in the breast pocket of his frock coat, and issued himself a stern warning. He could promise nothing but heartbreak to a woman like Angevine until he knew what had become of the one he loved first and best.

"You may see Creed Walker tonight," she said. "Do you remember him?"

"We never met, but I've heard of him."

"Then you've heard how he can be sometimes. They say it's the Kiowa blood in his veins."

"Sounds like you're warning me."

"It is wise to be prepared for the worst when Creed is around."

Torn left it at that and considered what he knew about Creed Walker.

Many years ago, Long Walker's wife had been taken by raiding Kiowas who, with their Comanche cousins, liked nothing better than to victimize the Five Civilized Tribes. After two months of captivity she was rescued by Creek lighthorse and returned safe and reasonably sound to her loving husband's arms. Seven months later, Creed entered the world; there could be no doubt his sire was a Kiowa warrior. To Long's credit, he had treated the boy as he would his own. Everyone else in the Creek Nation followed his lead.

It became evident early on that Creed was more Kiowa than Creek. Even as a young child he was wild, violent, and subject to dangerous moods. He shunned school, church, the life of a farmer. The peaceful ways of the Creek were not for him. At thirteen, Creed ran away and disappeared into the lawless Unassigned Lands. Long searched for him, as did the lighthorse. He could not be found. A year passed, and it was assumed he was either dead or running with the Kiowas.

But Creed returned. A boy had run away, a man came back, bigger, stronger, wilder than before. He did not stay for long. In the years to come, he never did. People feared him, and rightly so. His was the vicious arrogance of a wolf in a flock of sheep. He refused to wear the shackles of civilized behavior and spent most of his time in the wild country. It was rumored he did evil things, but, as far as Torn knew, no one had been able to produce solid evidence to that effect.

"I heard about what happened last night," said Angevine. "That poor woman. And then I got word Creed was back. I couldn't help but wonder if he . . . It isn't very fair, is it, Clay? But when someone dies, my first thought is: Creed Walker did it. And sometimes, late at night, when I hear a strange sound, I'm afraid it's him."

"Has he shown any interest in you?"

"Not particularly. But . . . well, you know."

"The Creek version of the boogie man."

She laughed. "Something like that."

"Why do you live alone, Angevine?"

She gave him a long, intense look.

"I'm waiting for the right man to come along."

"Must be a lot of young men with their caps set for you."

"But none of them is the right man."

"One of them could be, if you gave him a chance."

"I see." She sounded hurt.

Angry at himself, Torn clammed up.

A while later, in a firm tone of voice, she said, "I knew the right man the first time I laid eyes on him."

He pulled back on the reins and stopped the horse.

"What's wrong?" she asked, innocently.

"That last remark."

"Do you want it stricken from the record, Your Honor?"

"Now, look . . ."

"I *am* looking. But you're not looking at me."

He did, and it was a big mistake. She touched his cheek. Her face was very close to his and he could feel her warm breath, a sweet intoxication.

"I fell in love with you years ago, Clay Torn," she whispered. "It's easy to fall in, and so hard to climb back out. I haven't tried. I never will try."

"Angevine . . ."

"I know. You can't let go of her. And I can't let go of you. You should know how I feel."

She kissed him, lightly, her lips just brushing his.

"We'd better go on," he said thickly.

"We have time."

He saw passion blaze in her eyes. She kissed him again, harder this time. All the lonely years trailing behind him rushed up and gave him a shove, and he put his arms around her and stole her sweet breath away.

Then he heard the drumroll of a galloping horse, hellbent for election down the Texas Road.

Rougher than intended, he pushed her away. The Colt Peacemaker was in his hand; he wasn't conscious of drawing it. Twisting around on the buggy's seat, he thumbed the hammer back, his finger tight on the trigger.

A young man he didn't know thundered past on a foam-flecked buckskin, waving and whooping.

"That's John Drew," said Angevine, sounding peeved.

"One of those young men you mentioned. They'll all be there tonight. John will pester me for every dance."

The moment was lost. Torn regained his senses, flicked harness leather, and got things moving again.

CHAPTER 15

THE COUNCIL HOUSE WAS A LONG, LOW STRUCTURE, bigger than a barn, built of pine logs, with a roofed arbor on all four sides. Lanterns hung from every other upright supporting the arbor roof. Wagons and carriages were parked under the trees, and rows of horses were tethered to picket ropes.

As the night was warm, the tall windows and wide double doors on all four sides of the council house were open. Festive sounds poured out into the night. Men with guitars, fiddles, and harmonicas provided the music. They played "breakdowns" for the most part, throwing in an occasional reel. Tables were lined up along the walls, leaving the middle of the vast room open for a dance floor. The dancing did not stop.

Creeks from miles around had come to celebrate the marriage of two of their own, but everyone had been invited, and quite a few railroaders, cowboys, and whites from town had come. So had the bootleggers—dark, bearded characters with furtive eyes who conducted their business out under the trees, just beyond the throw of lantern light. They sold their moonshine by the drink, and their customers gladly paid the price. Everyone turned a blind eye to the proceedings. It made Torn wonder why they even kept the law against the sale and consumption of hard liquor on the books.

Angevine went off to help with the cooking, and Torn, finding a place at one of the tables, settled down to watch the festivities. Later, Angevine sought him out and asked him to dance with her. He declined. He had last danced at a cotillion in Charleston with Melony Hancock. The cotillion had been held in honor of volunteers like himself about to ride off to war. The memory of that occasion, his last night with Melony, never failed to cut deep, like the stroke of a saber, and he knew he would not dance again unless it was with the woman he had loved and lost and looked for all these years.

Doc Crane spotted Torn and came over to sit beside him.

"I admire these people," said Crane. "Their indomitable spirit. They get more than their fair share of grief and hardship, but you won't catch them long in the face. They don't want to bother anybody. They just want to live their lives in their own way, with a quiet, simple dignity."

"Sometimes life just won't leave you alone," said Torn.

"Judge, we've only met a couple of times," said the sawbones, "but I heard a lot about you, and I think I know the kind of man you are. You're as honest as they come. Which is the reason I have to admit I'm disappointed in you."

"Why?"

"Well, since you ask, I will tell you. You were holding

something back today at the inquest."

"Was I?"

Doc Crane's gravelly voice grated on Torn's conscience. "You didn't tell everything you knew. You left something out of your testimony."

"Nothing important."

"Now, now. You know it is not up to a witness to decide what is important and what isn't."

Torn felt like a criminal caught in the act, and he didn't like the feeling. Doc Crane had attended the inquest, and he had the nose of a bloodhound when it came to sniffing out corruption.

And that, mused Torn forlornly, *is what it amounts to.* He had avoided any mention of Judge Ronan in his testimony. A favor for a favor. Cronyism—there was no other word for it.

Torn squirmed, expecting Doc Crane to press the issue. To his surprise, the crusty old sawbones let him off the hook, changing the subject.

"Any idea who might have killed that poor woman?"

"No."

"Creed Walker has been seen in these parts. More than a few espouse the notion he did the deed. Bad timing on his part, if he didn't."

Torn did not reply. Doc Crane packed and lit a pipe before speaking again.

"Poor woman. A year from now few will remember. The community should be outraged, but it isn't. Morbid fascination, yes, but nary a whiff of outrage. Come the sabbath, the preachers will piously singe Miss O'Keefe's lost soul with fire and brimstone. They will employ her as an example of the reward awaiting those who live in sin. The flock will lap it up; my dear wife included. She has a theory of her own, by the way. One you might expect from a good Christian. That the man who butchered Miss O'Keefe was deranged, and that he was so because he suffered from syphilis, which he contracted from Miss O'Keefe. So you see, Miss O'Keefe is solely responsible for her own tragic end. Very tidy, don't you think? It certainly lets society off the hook."

"You sound bitter."

"Do I? I don't wonder. I have observed humanity for many years, and it seldom fails to disappoint me. Do you think there might be a connection between Big Mike's murder and Miss O'Keefe's?"

"If there is, I don't see it. You're a man of ideas. Have any regarding who might have wanted Big Mike dead?"

Doc Crane puffed on his pipe a moment. "He did not confide in me, so I'm afraid I don't know what he was working on. Big Mike was the kind of man who hoed his own row. I can't tell you *who* killed him, but I do know *what* killed him."

"What?"

"The deplorable condition of law and order in the Nations. The tribes have given the white man right-of-way for his railroads and emigrant trails, but they insist that only tribal law can be applied. Well, I'm sorry to say that Indian law is ill-equipped to deal with the crime the white man brings with him."

"How do you mean?"

"It's too fair, too slow. Big Mike had to go before the tribal council to get a warrant if he wanted to arrest someone. The tribal elders are wise men, but they are also compassionate men, and compassion has no place in the law."

Torn smiled. "It doesn't?"

"No. Because fair play only works among honorable men. And most white men are not honorable. Let me give you an example. A couple of years ago a Creek man, a farmer with a wife and family, was found guilty of killing another man in an argument over the ownership of a hog. He was sentenced to death, but given a choice as to the method and date of execution. As it was time for spring planting, he got permission to return home for a month to till and sow his fields, so that his family would not be left cropless and destitute. The man went home, did his planting, and a month later saddled his horse and reported to the execution site. Now, can you name me one white man who would have done that?"

"I honestly can't think of one, right off."

"My point is that Big Mike had to stem the tide of lawlessness in North Fork Town with his hands tied behind his back. He was Creek, and could do no less than abide by Creek law. Which is why Long Walker asked you to take over for him, and why I'm glad you did."

"I don't follow."

"Theoretically, you must abide by that same law. But what I like about you, Judge, is your propensity for ignoring the laws that don't suit you. You know that law and justice are sometimes two different things, and it's justice that you're after. So if you can't get justice playing by the rules, you make a new set of rules."

Angevine arrived at the table. Doc Crane, always the gentleman, stood. Torn did, too, reading the anxiety on her face, tightening the corners of her eyes and mouth.

"What is it?" he asked.

She pointed and he looked across the council house.

A man stood in a doorway, and a hush fell over the room. Torn had never laid eyes on Creed Walker, but he knew he was seeing the notorious renegade now. Lamplight glimmered in the man's cruel eyes and off the blade of the long knife in his belt.

CHAPTER

16

CREED WALKER'S ARRIVAL PUT A DAMPER ON THE FES-
tivities; the people were afraid of him. Creed enjoyed being
feared. He nurtured the image. He wore a sleeveless deer-
skin vest, fringed buckskin leggins, and tall cavalry boots.
His black hair was long and square-cut. This, Torn noticed,
was in sharp contrast to the hair of the civilized Creeks,
which as a rule was trimmed short. In addition to a hunting
knife, he wore a sidegun in an Army-issue flap holster.

"Those boots and that holster," murmured Doc Crane.
"I wonder if he killed for them."

"I was wondering the same thing," said Torn.

"That's the problem with Creed. No one has ever actually seen him commit a crime. But every stolen horse,
ambush shooting, and unsolved robbery is laid at his door-
step. If something bad happens in the Creek Nation, Creed
Walker is blamed. Why, they even say he rides with Kiowa
renegades against his own people."

"Who's the woman?"

"She's known as Spanish Red. Part Creek, part Mexican. Notorious in her own right. She works on Broken Wagon. Though she has Creek blood, she is not made to feel welcome by the tribe. Her profession offends the people. The Creeks will tolerate prostitution—with so many cowboys and cavalrymen, it is a necessary evil—but they don't like one of their own debasing herself."

Spanish Red wore a scarlet dress accentuating every lush curve of her body. She had more moves than a sidewinder. Her jet-black hair was done up with stickpins and her plain features were painted with rouge. She sashayed on Creed's muscular arm.

Creed steered her across the council house. He was a big man, but in spite of his brawn he moved with a menacing grace. He seemed to have picked Torn out of the crowd, and made a beeline for the table.

"So, you must be the new law," he said, grinning. There was nothing friendly about that grin. "A tall man dressed in black. You want to arrest me, maybe?"

"Should I?"

"That's for you to find out."

"Polishing the bad image, I see," said Torn.

Creed's eyes narrowed. "This is Creek land. A Creek should be the law here, not a white man. That's the problem with the old men who say they have the right to run tribal affairs. Little by little, they give away their power to the whites. Pretty soon, they will have no say in what goes on here."

"If you had your way," said Doc Crane, "you'd shut down the railroad and the cattle trail and shoot every white man who set foot in the Creek Nation."

"You know me, don't you?" sneered Creed.

"Problem is," smiled Crane, "you're half white yourself."

Creed hawked and spat. "That's for my white mother, and every drop of white blood in my veins."

"Well," said Torn, "you could cut your wrists and let all that white blood out. You might feel better, and I know everybody else would."

Doc Crane laughed softly. Creed was not amused. He stared at Torn, hooded eyes unblinking, dull and black like the eyes of a doll.

"I smell whiskey," he said, and turned to go.

"No trouble, Creed," warned Torn.

"I come to drink, to dance." He leered at Spanish Red. "And to do other things. I did not come for trouble. But if I change my mind, I'll let you know."

He walked away, Spanish Red on his arm.

Doc Crane took his leave. Angevine hung onto Torn's arm, and he could tell she was frightened.

"I wish he hadn't come," she said. "He's a bad man."

"I've seen worse."

"I'm glad Long isn't here. It hurts him so, the way Creed acts. I wish Creed would stay away."

"You don't have to be afraid of him, Angevine."

"I'm not, as long as you're here."

Torn kept a close watch on Creed. In spite of the renegade's assurances, he expected trouble.

It wasn't long in coming. Creed insisted on dancing with Mary Paige. Understandably, her husband-to-be was primed to protest, but calmer heads prevailed, as everybody preferred a wedding to a funeral.

Creed was no dancer, but he was quick and agile, and he whirled Mary around with malicious enthusiasm, out of step with the rhythm of the reel. No one else danced—

no one cared to get in Creed Walker's way. Torn heard no laughter now.

So intent was he on keeping a wary eye on Creed, that Torn overlooked the arrival of two troopers from Fort Gibson. He first saw them hovering around Spanish Red while Creed manhandled Mary Paige. Their presence did not do much for his peace of mind.

Horse soldiers were a rough and rowdy lot. Theirs was a hard life, by turns tediously dull and extremely dangerous. Torn assumed they had passes authorizing their absence from the fort. He had seen more than a few soldiers in North Fork Town.

These two were paying Spanish Red the kind of attention she was accustomed to. Their advances did not seem to bother her.

But Creed Walker was bothered.

The reel ended at a most inopportune moment. Creed released Mary, who was some the worse for her ordeal. Her future husband rushed to her side, putting his arms around her and firing an angry look at Creed. Creed laughed in his face and turned to see one of the troopers mauling Spanish Red's generous breasts.

Roaring like a bull on the prod, Creed charged.

Torn was up and moving in the same second.

Creed peeled the soldier off Spanish Red and hurled him ten feet. The cavalryman went skidding across a floor worn smooth by countless feet. Spanish Red laughed at this spectacle. The second trooper took two backward steps. Creed mistook this for retreat, and turned his rage on Spanish Red, slapping her across the face. The blow sounded like the crack of a bullwhip. Spanish Red spun and fell.

"You goddamned dog-eater," growled the second trooper. "Didn't know she was your own private stock."

Creed faced him, saw the Schofield revolver in the soldier's hand, and realized his error. The trooper was in a position to kill him before he got the flap of his holster undone and his own pistol into play. Several women in the crowd cried alarm, anticipating a killing.

Creed snarled and lunged barehanded at the trooper.

This move caught Torn by surprise. Charging a man with a gun was tantamount to suicide. It was incredibly brave or remarkably stupid, depending on your point of view. Torn learned a great deal about Creed Walker at that moment.

Torn had been homing in on the trooper with the gun. He'd read the man better than Creed had and expected the draw. But when Creed charged, Torn altered the angle of his onslaught by a few degrees, blindsiding Creed. His punch hammered Creed into the ground.

Out of the corner of his eye he saw the trooper's gun swing in his direction. Lashing out, he grabbed the barrel, twisted and pushed at the same time, plowed into the cavalryman, and drove an elbow into the man's face. The trooper crumpled, his knees turned to rubber, blood gushing from a broken nose. Torn wrenched the Schofield out of his grasp.

He stepped away then, just enough to put some room between himself and Creed and the soldiers. Shifting the Schofield to his left hand, he drew his Colt Peacemaker. The first trooper had stopped sliding. Now he got up, slowly and painfully. Torn covered him with the Colt, Creed and the other trooper with the Schofield.

"Throw your gun away."

The first trooper stared blankly at Torn, as though he wasn't sure Torn was talking to him. But when his gaze fell to the Colt aimed at his heart, he understood. Considering his options, he hesitated.

"Don't be a fool," snapped Torn. "You won't live to regret it."

He longed for the Fox scattergun. He'd carried it since his first night making the rounds, but tonight it stood in the jail's gunrack. Nothing surpassed a sawed-off shotgun for persuading a man to see reason.

The trooper made the right decision. He unbuckled his belt and let it drop.

"Kick it away," said Torn.

The soldier complied.

Creed was on hands and knees, groggily shaking his head. He saw the second trooper groveling on the floor, hands covering his face, blood leaking through his fingers. A growl welled up in Creed's throat. He gathered himself and lunged. Torn's kick caught him in midair. Creed rolled and came to his feet with the hunting knife in hand. Torn was impressed. A kick in the guts seemed to have little effect on Creed Walker.

He cocked the Schofield and drew a bead on the renegade.

"Try that on me and I'll kill you where you stand."

He was half-convinced he would have to do just that, since Creed had already jumped a man pointing a gun at him.

But Creed froze in his tracks.

"Get rid of the knife and the gun," said Torn.

Creed threw the knife away. He shed the gunbelt. All the while he stared at Torn with those dull, black eyes, his features set in stone, betraying no hint of emotion.

"You broke my nose!" gargled the trooper on the floor.

"Get up."

The cavalryman obeyed. He stood bent over, swaying, dripping blood.

"You're under arrest," Torn told him. "You too, Creed."

"You're not going to lock me in some iron cage," growled Creed, big fists clenched.

"Jail or boot hill. Your decision."

"What about me?" asked the first trooper.

"All you did was polish the floor. You can leave."

"Let Rutledge go. The Indian started it."

"He pointed a pistol at me. I'm not in a forgiving mood."

"You don't understand, mister. We . . . we ain't supposed to be here in the first place. We could be shot for leaving the fort without a pass."

"I doubt that," said Torn.

The trooper turned pale. "I mean it, mister. You just don't know . . ."

"You could always desert."

"O'Malley!" howled Rutledge furiously, spewing blood. "Don't leave me in the damn jail to rot!"

"A Rexrode mule's got more brains than you, Rutledge," replied O'Malley, disgusted with the way things were going. "Mister, can I at least take my pistol?"

"No."

With a curt nod, O'Malley pushed through the crowd and headed for the nearest door.

Torn motioned with the guns, indicating to Creed and Rutledge that they, too, should start moving.

"Let's go, gents," he said. "The party's over."

CHAPTER 17

THE DAWN ACCOMPANIED LONG WALKER INTO NORTH Fork Town. He trudged up the Texas Road, his movements stiff with age, relying heavily on his hickory cane as he navigated the wide expanse of rutted dust.

Torn saw him coming from the porch of the stone jailhouse. He watched a man on horseback and another in a wagon give Long the right of way and speak respectfully to the old chief. But Long did not seem to notice them. He was lost in melancholy thought.

Postponing the breakfast he had planned to get across the street at the Keystone, Torn went back inside and waited for Long's arrival. He offered him a cup of coffee, but Long graciously declined. Standing before the desk, Long's attention strayed to the strap-iron cells. One held Rutledge. The trooper sat, slump-shouldered and perfectly miserable, on the narrow bunk. His face was swollen and discolored. Doc Crane had set and bandaged his nose, but he was still swimming in a sea of pain—and in a great deal of doubt regarding his future.

Creed occupied the other cell. Stretched out on the bunk, he did not respond to the sound of his father's voice. He appeared to be sleeping, but Torn knew he was only pretending. A change in the rhythm of his breathing betrayed him.

Torn motioned to one of the chairs facing the desk and asked Long to sit. Long shook his head.

"When I heard what happened last night at the council house I was angry. They told me you had arrested Creed, and I said this was good, that Creed did the devil's work. He brought fear and violence upon his own people. I said the Creek Nation did not want him and I was ashamed to admit he was my son."

Torn did not know what to say. He felt as uncomfortable as Long appeared to be himself.

"Now I am ashamed of myself," continued Long. "Of my angry words last night. I spoke without thinking."

"I think you were fully justified."

"No. For a father to say such things about his son is wrong."

"You're a good man."

"I am old and weak." Long gravely shook his head again. "I have come to ask you to release my son."

"Are you sure that's what you want?"

"I am sure."

"I'll tell him to stay out of North Fork Town if you want me to."

As he spoke, Torn glanced at the cell containing Creed. He expected a defiant response, but Creed lay unmoving on the bunk.

"That would only lead to bloodshed," sighed Long. "He would take it as a challenge. He would not stay away. One of you would have to kill the other."

"All right. I'll cut him loose."

"Many thanks. Please understand. My dear wife bore him. He is her flesh and blood."

"You don't need to explain."

"Indulge an old man. I feel responsible. It is my fault she was taken captive by the Kiowas."

"You couldn't have prevented it, from what I've heard."

"It is a husband's responsibility to protect his wife. I did not protect her, so I must protect her son. This is the least I can do. I owe her that much."

It shocked Torn to realize that he and Long Walker shared similar burdens of guilt. He felt responsible for Melony Hancock's abduction by Yankee deserters at the end of the war. There was nothing he could have done to prevent it—he'd been hundreds of miles away, running for his life after his escape from Point Lookout—but he had carried the burden for ten years and would not lay it down until he had located Melony. He found it easy to advise Long Walker not to blame himself for the abduction and rape of his wife, and impossible to exonerate himself in his own case.

Taking the cell key from a desk drawer, Torn crossed the room and unlocked the door to Creed's iron cage. The hinges grated, a high-pitched shriek of iron; a nerve-jangling noise loud enough to wake the dead. But Creed Walker did not even twitch.

"You're free to go," said Torn. "Stop hiding from your father. Stand up and face him like a man."

The goading worked. Creed rose from the bunk in one fluid motion.

"He is not my father. My father was a great Kiowa warrior."

"It's your loss that this man is not your true father,"

replied Torn. "But he has treated you like a son. He was not obliged by Creek law to do so."

He went back to the desk, took Creed's knife, gun, and gunbelt from the drawer. Creed checked the pistol's cylinder.

"I want the bullets."

"Forget it."

"You are a thief and a coward."

"Creed, don't," implored Long.

"You can't tell me what to do, old man."

Soft-spoken, Torn said, "Take your weapons and get out of my sight."

"I will get more bullets," said Creed belligerently.

He brushed Long on purpose as he made for the door, shoving the old man off balance. Torn put his temper on short rein, out of respect for Long, and let Creed go.

"I will pray for his soul," said Long sadly.

Torn thought prayers would be better spent on everyone else in the Nations as long as Creed Walker was loose. He couldn't shake the feeling that releasing the man was a mistake. Mad dogs had to put down, sooner or later, and the sooner the better.

CHAPTER 18

Long Walker had not been gone long when Torn heard horses checked in front of the jail. Stepping out to investigate, he was confronted by three cavalrymen. One wore a lieutenant's bars, another a sergeant's chevrons, and the third was a private. The lieutenant dismounted, tendered his reins to the trooper, and peeled off calfskin gauntlets as he mounted the boardwalk.

"I am Lieutenant Stride, sir," he informed Torn. "I am looking for two soldiers."

He spoke with a clipped British accent; quite a few officers in the United States Army were foreign-born. Mercenaries or remittance men, some were competent while others were strutting martinets. Torn wondered to which category Lt. Stride belonged.

"I have one of the men you're looking for," he said. "I can't tell you about the other."

"Indeed." Stride gave Torn a steely and rather superior

once-over. "You say you have one. Under arrest?"

"Yes."

"His name?"

"Rutledge."

"The charge?"

"He pointed a gun at me."

Stride fingered a sweeping mustache, which when combined with tawny sideburns and dense brows covered most of a long, sallow face. A trim, erect man, his uniform was resplendent despite a coat of dust. He wore jackboots, fancy spurs and a short, yellow-edged cape. His Allien dress helmet was adorned with braided lines and a yak hair plume dyed red. A saber was belted on his left side.

"What, may I ask, was his reason for doing so?" asked Stride.

"Ask him."

Stride pursed thin, bloodless lips. "Is it your intention to press the issue?"

"That depends."

"On?"

"How much trouble he's in already."

"Privates O'Malley and Rutledge were missing at roll call. Colonel Finney ordered me to apprehend them, as they are in my troop. He suggested North Fork Town as the most promising place to begin my search."

"Good guess."

"I venture to say bad whiskey and worse women were ingredients in the downfall of Trooper Rutledge."

"That's what your men come here for, Lieutenant."

"This town has lured many a good soldier down a path of debauchery and ruin, sir."

"You don't approve of whiskey or women, I take it."

Detecting a trace of sarcasm in Torn's comment, Stride stiffened.

"A good soldier must be a Spartan, morally as well as physically."

"What happens to Rutledge?"

"He may face court-martial, at Colonel Finney's discretion, under Article 61 of the Articles of War, for being absent without leave."

Torn remembered O'Malley lamenting that they might be shot. Technically it was so, but such draconian measures were not usually employed these days. At worst, Rutledge—and O'Malley, if caught—faced a long stretch in the brig.

"I would like to speak to Private Rutledge alone for a moment," said Stride.

Torn took the cell key out of his pocket and gave it to the lieutenant.

"His gun's in the desk. I'll wait out here."

Stride stepped inside, spurs singing against the floorboards.

The sergeant climbed down off his horse and flexed his stumpy legs. He was a beefy, red-faced individual with the salty look of an old campaigner. Taking off his forage cap, he wiped the sweat off a shaved head with the sleeve of his tunic.

"Where's Big Mike?" he asked.

"Dead."

The sergeant grinned. "What a shame. Who the hell are you?"

"A friend of his."

"Friend to a lousy half-breed?" The sergeant turned to the still-mounted trooper. "I ask you, Murphy, is that any way for a white man to act?"

The trooper shrugged, sliding an apologetic glance Torn's way. He wanted no part of this.

The sergeant pulled a Bowie knife out of his boot to

slice a corner off a plug of tobacco.

"Damn breeds are worse than a fullblood copperbelly, to my way of thinking," declared the sergeant. "They get to thinking they're better than they are. Breed men are cowards. A breed kid is a worse thief than a camp dog. And breed women are whores, every one. What do you think about that, friend?"

"I think you're looking for a fight."

Sliding the knife back into his boot, the sergeant laughed. "You think you can take me, you just . . ."

Torn threw a punch at the man's head. It was a feint. The three-striper fell for it, lifting his arms to block the blow. Torn's fist slammed into the sergeant's paunch. The man doubled over, spitting out his quid. Torn's knee came up into his face. The sergeant landed on his back in the street. His horse shied away. Grunting like a pig, the cavalryman tried to get up. Torn kicked him in the head, the tip of his boot connecting squarely with the point of the chin. The sergeant went out like a candle in a strong wind, spreadeagled in the dust.

"You don't fight fair!" complained the trooper.

"I fight to win."

"What's the meaning of this?"

Stride stormed out of the jail, Rutledge behind him. The lieutenant was carrying the trooper's gunbelt. He scowled at the unconscious sergeant, then at Torn.

"You need to teach your sergeant some manners," said Torn.

"I see you've given the first lesson. I'll have you know Sergeant Jurgen is the regiment's champion pugilist. This should demonstrate to him the folly of underestimating his opponent." Stride took the reins of his horse from Murphy. "Retrieve the sergeant's horse, Private."

"Yes, sir!" Murphy wheeled his mount and pursued Jurgen's horse, which was heading down the street at a lope.

Stride noticed the boardwalks filling with spectators, drawn by the action in front of the jail. He draped Rutledge's gunbelt over the horn of his McClellan saddle and mounted up. Rutledge stepped respectfully wide around Torn.

"Trooper Rutledge tells me he and O'Malley left their horses in the woods near the council house," said Stride. "He says he told you. Where is the horse?"

"I don't know. I looked for it. My guess is O'Malley took both horses."

Stride nodded. "For a hard ride to Mexico. Well, we shall add theft of government property to the charge of desertion. Trooper Rutledge will have to walk back to Fort Gibson."

"Go to the livery. John Eagle will loan you a horse."

"Rutledge will walk," said Stride.

"That's ten miles, Lieutenant."

"I know how far it is. You need not concern yourself. Trooper Rutledge is the army's business now."

Stride uncapped his canteen and dribbled water on Jurgen's face. The sergeant sputtered and came to. Murphy returned with his horse, and Rutledge helped the groggy three-striper into the saddle. Jurgen looked blankly at Torn, like he didn't even recognize him and couldn't remember what had transpired. All the fight had gone out of him.

Torn watched them go. Three riders and one afoot. He felt sorry for Rutledge.

As he turned to enter the jail, he heard his name called. Windy Smith was crossing the street in a hurry, hitching along on his game leg.

"Judge Torn," he gasped, bent over with hands on knees, heaving in air—it was a handsome run from the freight office. "Just rolled in from McAlester. I come straight to you . . ."

"What's wrong?"

"Found a body in the brush near the road. Just a handful of miles out of town."

"A body? Who?"

Windy gulped. "Ain't a purty sight. Varmints been at her. It was the buzzards led me to her."

"Her?" Torn felt cold clean through.

"Don't know her name, but I seen her before. She worked the line." Windy blushed furiously. "Not that I visit Virgin Alley, you understand. Lord A'mighty, if I did, my wife would break my skull with a skillet. She's a fullblood Creek, and Creek women are . . ."

"The dead woman—what was she wearing?"

"Well, let's see. A green shirt, green hat. Some thin black gloves with the fingers cut out . . ."

"Nellie Bond," said Torn.

CHAPTER 19

WINDY SMITH AGREED TO TAKE TORN TO THE PLACE where he had discovered the body. Torn stopped by Doc Crane's. Crane wearily agreed to be along shortly. He would come out in a buckboard, so that the body could be transported back to town. Torn hired a horse at John Eagle's livery.

"I wanted to bring her in with me," said Windy, apologetic. "But I . . . I jis' couldn't."

"Don't worry about it," said Torn.

As they drew near the spot, several buzzards rose from the timber, hurling themselves into the white afternoon sky with an angry flapping of wings. A funny look on his face, Windy checked his horse.

"Don't reckon I want to see it again, Judge. Once is one time too many."

Torn nodded.

Dismounting, he ground-hitched his horse and braced

himself. His approach through the underbrush dispersed a few more buzzards. One remained, perched adamantly on Nellie Bond's bloody chest. Torn yelled. The buzzard resentfully hopped off the body, but refused to take flight until Torn hurled a stone.

Stomach churning, Torn turned away from the sight. In his time he had seen a lot of death. On the battlefield, men riddled by musket fire, torn apart by cannon balls and grapeshot. In Point Lookout Prison, he had seen disease and starvation slowly suck the life out of fellow prisoners of war. Out here on the frontier he had seen the remains of men and women tortured and scalped by Indians. In spite of all that experience, he could not now look upon Nellie Bond with much equanimity.

Like Katy O'Keefe, she had been butchered.

"You okay, Judge?" called Windy from the Texas Road.

Torn's shout had alarmed him. He stood in his stirrups to peer through the sumac and redhaw.

Torn moved so the freight driver could see him and raised a hand in an all's-well gesture. Taking a deep breath, he turned back to the body.

Nellie Bond's head was completely detached from the body. The upper torso had been cut open. Coyotes had dragged the internal organs out of the body cavity. Flies swarmed in the terrible wounds. A sour stench permeated the hot, still air. The corpse was deteriorating rapidly in the summer heat.

The body lay in a small clearing. Torn searched the ground for sign. Nellie had put up a struggle. She had crawled, or been dragged, about twenty feet. There were a lot of bloodstains, and the tracks of a man wearing square-toed boots.

Torn pressed on through the brush. He found the hoof-prints of a shod horse, and one person on foot. The latter had obviously been Nellie—the footprints were quite small. She was running. Here she fell, got up to run again, weaving through the brush, tearing her clothes. The horse was held to a lope, the best gait the rider could achieve working through the woods. On open ground the chase would have been over a lot sooner.

Clearly, Nellie had been running for her life, pursued by a man on horseback. Closing in, the killer had jumped off his horse and committed the murder.

The killer's boot prints told Torn very little. There was nothing distinctive about them, or the tracks made by the killer's mount.

The tracks of woman and horse led Torn along the west rim of a steep, vine-choked ravine. In time, the tracks separated. Torn followed Nellie's sign back to the Texas Road. She was still running—had run off the road and into the brush. Cut off by the ravine, she had veered south along its rim, eventually angling back toward the Texas Road.

Windy came down the road with Torn's horse in tow. Torn signaled for him to hold where he was, and retraced his steps to the spot where the tracks of horse and woman merged near the ravine. This time he backtracked the horse and again ended up at the road.

So Nellie had been walking along the road, in the direction of McAlester. The rider had come from the direction of North Fork Town. She had started to run. The horseman had angled off the road to intercept her. He had run her down and murdered her.

Back at the road, Torn took his reins from Windy and bleakly surveyed the woods on both sides of the road. Not a breath of wind stirred the trees. It was hot and humid; his clothes were drenched with sweat.

"Sure wish she'd seen fit to take the stage or the train

to wherever she was going," said Windy, morose. "Ain't safe for a woman alone out here, what with all the renegades and road agents. Reckon she didn't have the fare."

Torn shook his head. He had given Nellie Bond money out of his own pocket, so that she could afford transportation.

Had she spent the money on something else? Whiskey or opium, perhaps? It hardly seemed logical that she would opt to walk all the way to McAlester from North Fork Town, a distance of more than thirty miles. Maybe she'd expected to hitch a ride; the Texas Road was usually well-traveled. Maybe she had counted on this, and kept the money for a grubstake to help her get started elsewhere. Possibly, she still had the money on her. Torn was curious, but he didn't really feel up to searching the body right now.

"So what do you think, Judge?" asked Windy. "Think renegade Injuns done it?"

"I don't know."

The horse had been steelshod, but many of the Indians of the Civilized Tribes put iron on their mounts. All he was sure of was that the man who had murdered Nellie Bond was the same one who had murdered Katy O'Keefe. It could have been an Indian. He hated to admit it, but as far as he knew, it could have been anybody.

"Won't never be able to pass by here without getting all jabber-jawed," said Windy, apprehensively studying this stretch of road. "Believe in ghosts, Judge?"

"I don't know."

"Well, I sure do. A mighty strange thing happened at Fort Sill, west of here, a couple years ago. That was when Satank and his Kiowas were raising cain. A yellowleg patrol got ambushed. A young shavetail fresh out of West Point was leading the patrol. He was engaged to be married to the commandant's daughter. She was the belle of Fort Sill, they say. And when her lieutenant rode out the gate for the last time, she swore her undying love and loyalty to him.

"The Kiowas killed most of the soldiers right off, but they took the lieutenant prisoner. Tortured him something terrible. They say the Apaches are bad about that, but for my money there ain't nothin' on God's good green earth more unadulterated mean than a Kiowa.

"The whole garrison rode out to rescue the lieutenant, but they never found him. Weeks passed. The commandant had to report the young officer as missing and presumed dead.

"His daughter grieved something fierce, but she was young; she got over it. Maybe a little quicker than some thought proper. Other young officers started courting her. Their attentions soon caused her to forget the oath she'd sworn to her lost love.

"Now, one night they were set to have a dance, and the young lady had no intention of sitting at home, all dressed up in mourning black. The shivaree was in full swing when the door flew open and in stepped the young lieutenant.

"He was dead, Judge. Dead for weeks. And not just run-of-the-mill dead, but with the life tortured out of him inch by screaming inch. He walked right up to the young woman, cursed her for being unfaithful, and the flames of Hell crackled in his voice. When he put his hands on her she screamed and screamed. She lost her mind; went stark raving mad—crazy as a horse with a stomach full of locoweed. The last few weeks of her life she hardly stopped screaming. The lieutenant, he'd been long dead, so you can't say he died that night, but they picked what was left of his mortal remains off the dance floor and buried him deep."

Windy Smith shuddered and glanced over his shoulder, in the direction of Nellie Bond's body.

"That's quite a tale, Windy," said Torn.

"Ain't it?" Windy laughed, nervous and self-conscious. "I just can't help but think I'll be hearing her screams, when on some quiet night I pass by here."

Torn gazed at the dark and silent woods.

"Maybe you will," he said.

CHAPTER 20

THE CREAK AND RATTLE OF A BUCKBOARD TURNED their attention north, and they saw Doc Crane rolling down the Texas Road.

Torn took him to the body.

"I see the coyotes got to her," said Crane tersely.

"Need me to do anything, Doc?"

"No."

Relieved, Torn walked away, following the tracks back to the ravine, thinking he might have missed something. Something *was* missing; he just couldn't put his finger on it.

When he spotted the carpetbag wedged between the trunks of scrub willows halfway down the flank of the ravine, he realized what that something was.

He'd seen Nellie Bond with that carpetbag the day she left North Fork Town. Fleeing for her life, she had dropped it, and it had rolled down the slope.

Picking his way down the steep incline, Torn retrieved the bag, and climbed back to the rim. He unstrapped the bag and opened it. Going through the personal effects of the dead made him uneasy, but it was something he had to do. He wasn't sure what he was looking for; something that would explain why Nellie Bond had to die. Something that would make sense of these senseless murders.

The carpetbag was stuffed with clothes, and satin and lace fineries that had seen better days. He found a half empty bottle of cheap rye whiskey, a hairbrush, a hand mirror, a small book of Psalms bound in red leather, and a letter. The envelope was blank, unsealed.

He opened the letter. No date, no salutation. The handwriting was neat and precise.

By the time you get this I will be far away. You may find out I posted this in McAlester, but don't bother looking I'm not there. Why why did you do that to poor Katy you butcher. We will both carry the blame to our graves. May your soul rot in everlasting Hell. Mine will I am sure. I never thought money meant so much to you that you would kill rather than part with ten thousand dollars. You are worse than I thought. Well now you will know you made a mistake. It was me not poor Katy. I wrote the letters. This time I will sign my name.

Nellie

P.S.
You won't get away with it, you bastard. I hope to see you hanged.

Torn read the letter through several times, then returned it to its envelope and put the envelope in an inside pocket of his black frock coat. Putting the rest of Nellie

Bond's belongings back in the carpetbag, he carried it to the road where Windy was waiting with the horses. The freight driver was sitting on his heels in the thin shade of his sorrel mare. Torn hooked the bag's handles over the horn of his saddle.

Doc Crane trudged out of the trees. His sleeves were rolled up, his arms smeared with dark blood and gore. He looked extremely tired as he threw his black grip into the buckboard and took a long drink of water from a canteen that had been lying on the seat. He swished the water around in his mouth and spat it out, watching the parched earth suck it up.

"Scavengers did a lot of damage," he said. "But I can safely say her throat was slashed. She was cut open, just like that other woman. My guess is it happened late yesterday." He looked at the buzzards describing lazy circles in the sun-bleached sky. "I brought a couple of blankets and some rope. I'll need help."

"You hold the horses, Windy," said Torn. "I'll give Doc a hand."

Green around the gills, Windy nodded gratefully.

They wrapped Nellie Bond's remains in the blankets and loaded them into the back of the buckboard. Torn returned to the woods to retrieve her little green hat with its piece of yellow ribbon. This he secured beneath a fold in the blankets.

Doc Crane turned the buckboard around and headed back to town. Torn and Windy rode far enough behind to stay clear of the plume of dust thrown by the buckboard's wheels. Neither man spoke. Torn pondered Nellie's letter. He was certain the person to whom she had written the letter was the murderer. If only she had addressed it!

Certain elements of the letter were particularly intriguing. Ten thousand dollars. *I never thought money meant so much to you.* Who in North Fork Town had that kind of money? The hotel owner, Boone Sowerwine. The cattle buyer, John Moultrie. Judge Ronan was doing well for himself as an Indian trader. And it was rumored that Whispering Jack Capehart had a lot of money stashed away. Undoubtedly there were others.

Torn decided he could eliminate Moultrie and Ronan from this list of suspects. He had seen Moultrie in the French Lily at the time of Katy O'Keefe's murder. And Judge Ronan had obviously been otherwise engaged.

Nellie had also referred to previous letters. Torn knew she'd been blackmailing the murderer, but with what leverage? What did she know that was worth ten thousand dollars? Or worth killing for?

She had gambled that the victim of her extortion would not go to extremes. Gambled and lost. She had not known, until the murder of Katy O'Keefe, that she had picked the worst possible man to blackmail—a man with so little respect for human life that he found it easier to kill her than deal with her.

Torn had found his clue; it was beginning to make sense. But for all the letter told him, the killer's identity remained a mystery.

A gunshot rang out.

He checked his horse. So did Windy Smith. Up ahead, Doc Crane climbed harness leather to stop the two mules from pulling the buckboard. Two more shots, close together, splintered the hot, still afternoon. Windy pulled thoughtfully on his chin.

" 'Bout a mile yonder," he judged, nodding west. "T'other side of that rise."

Torn listened a moment for more gunfire, but there wasn't any more. Doc Crane turned on his seat.

"What do you figure?" he asked.

Torn knew it could be something as innocent as an Indian out hunting. Or it could be trouble. The Nations were a wild and lawless territory. He had enough trouble without buying into more, but curiosity conquered reason. He felt compelled to investigate.

"I'll go have a look," he said. "You two go on ahead. I'll catch up."

"Be careful," advised Crane. "I don't need any more business today."

Torn nodded and turned his horse off the Texas Road.

CHAPTER

21

REACHING THE CREST OF THE TREE-CLAD HILL, TORN looked down upon a stretch of prairie spotted with clumps of persimmons, as flat and hot as the bottom of an iron skillet. He immediately spotted four men not far from the foot of the hill. Recognizing them, he urged his horse down the slope.

Lt. Stride and the trooper named Murphy were sitting their horses. Rutledge lay sprawled on his face, unmoving. Sergeant Jurgen had dismounted and was kneeling beside the body. As Torn emerged from the trees, Jurgen rose and turned, bringing his Sharps carbine to his shoulder.

Torn pulled back on the reins, his heart leaping into his throat. Jurgen had him dead to rights, but Stride goaded his horse in front of the three-striper, blocking his shot, snapping a curt order. The burly sergeant reluctantly lowered the carbine.

His hand resting on the butt of his Colt sidegun, Torn

put his horse into motion again.

"What's going on here?" he asked curtly.

"None of your business," growled Jurgen. "Butt out."

"That's quite enough, Sergeant," barked Stride.

Torn glanced at the body. Rutledge's blue tunic showed a dark, glistening stain of blood between the shoulder blades. Torn counted three bulletholes. He was dead.

"I don't miss," bragged Jurgen.

Torn had heard three shots; Rutledge had been struck three times—evidently Jurgen wasn't exaggerating his marksmanship.

"Why did you kill him?"

"He was trying to escape," said Stride.

Torn's smile was warm as winter.

"Trying to escape?" he echoed, every word shot through with skepticism.

"Sergeant Jurgen, in his own blunt way, is quite correct. This isn't your concern. It is army business."

Torn noticed Rutledge's gunbelt still draped over the pommel of the lieutenant's McClellan saddle.

"Let me get this straight. A man on foot, unarmed, made a break for it out in the middle of this open country. And instead of just riding him down, you shot him down."

"That's the long and short of it," sneered Jurgen.

Although cool and composed on the surface, Stride was becoming aggravated and his tone of voice betrayed him.

"Private Rutledge was under arrest. He was shot trying to escape. I gave the order. Sergeant Jurgen did his duty. I dare say I was within my rights."

Torn smelled a rat. True, army discipline was strict, the penalties for misconduct harsh, but this had the stench of murder to it.

He glanced at Murphy. The trooper appeared deeply agitated. What he had witnessed didn't sit well, but he was tight-lipped. Torn sensed he would not speak up in the presence of Stride.

"Murphy," said the lieutenant, "get down and help Sergeant Jurgen put the body across your saddle." Stride fastened those cold, black, soulless eyes on Torn. "If there is nothing further, sir, we shall proceed to Fort Gibson."

Torn realized there was nothing he could do. It *was* army business, and even a federal judge was powerless to interfere.

Worst of all, he felt partly to blame. If he hadn't locked Rutledge up, the man might have made it back in time for roll call, and none of this would have happened.

He glanced at Jurgen. Every time he looked at this man he saw Karl Schmidt, the sadistic Point Lookout guard who had dedicated himself to making Torn's sixteen months of captivity a living hell. Schmidt and Jurgen were cut from the same cloth; both men had a brutal disregard for human life. Both derived pleasure from meting out pain. Schmidt had been the most evil, the most morally bankrupt individual Torn had ever had the misfortune to meet. Now he was beginning to wonder if Jurgen wasn't one to give Schmidt a run for his money in that regard.

It's a good thing, thought Torn, *that I don't believe in reincarnation.*

He looked at the carbine in Jurgen's hands. Turning his back on a confirmed backshooter was no easy thing. The sergeant saw Torn's hesitation. He smiled a crooked, unpleasant smile.

"What's the matter?" leered Jurgen. "You look spooked."

Stride intervened. "Sergeant, boot that carbine and lend Murphy a hand."

Jurgen obeyed. As he and the trooper draped the body over Murphy's saddle, Torn neck-reined his horse and without another word proceeded back into the trees. He had an itch between his shoulder blades all the way, but exercised self-control and refrained from looking back until he reached cover. He thought it possible Jurgen might be watching, hoping to witness some show of fear on his part, and Torn refused to give the man the satisfaction.

A few yards into the trees, he stopped the horse and turned to look. The cavalrymen were heading north. Stride was in the lead, followed by Jurgen. Murphy walked, leading his horse, with Rutledge over the saddle.

Troubled, Torn headed up the wooded slope. Too many people were dying under mysterious circumstances. First Big Mike, then Katy O'Keefe and Nellie Bond, now Trooper Rutledge. Was there a connection?

Torn knew he had to find out. Fast.

CHAPTER

22

A CROWD WAS QUICK TO GATHER WHEN TORN, WINDY,
and Doc Crane arrived back in North Fork Town with
Nellie Bond's body. Windy had mentioned his grisly discovery at the freight company office beforehand, and the
word had spread like a prairie fire.

Doc Crane drove his buckboard straight to John Eagle's
livery. The ancient Creek forge-master had already started
on the coffin. In a matter of minutes the street was filled
with curious onlookers. The sun had set, and some of the
men carried lanterns to throw back the purple shadows of
twilight.

John Eagle helped Torn carry the blanket-wrapped body
into the livery. The crowd tagged along and Torn promptly
herded them back out. A dozen questions were hurled at
him. He raised his hands, gesturing for quiet.

"Her name was Nellie Bond. She worked on Broken
Wagon."

"Was she murdered?" one man asked.

"Yes."

"Who done it?" queried another.

"I don't know, yet."

"You better find him soon," said the first man grimly. "Our wives and children aren't safe until you do."

Torn understood their concern. All they knew was that someone was murdering women in their community, and doing it in a spectacularly brutal fashion. They didn't know what he knew: that the killer was only after the woman who had been blackmailing him.

"The murderer made a mistake when he killed Katy O'Keefe," he announced. "He meant to kill Nellie Bond. He's done what he set out to do."

"Maybe," muttered the first man, dubious. "Maybe not."

"If you're worried for your families, why aren't you at home protecting them?"

It was a point they could not argue. The crowd began to disperse. Doc Crane, shoulders slumped with fatigue, was on his way out of the livery. Torn asked him to wait a minute.

John Eagle had already put up his horse, and Torn found Nellie Bond's carpetbag still tied to the saddle. He carried the bag over to the old Creek forge-master, who was using an adz to square off a board destined to become part of the dead woman's coffin.

"This belonged to her," said Torn, not knowing quite what to do with the carpetbag.

John Eagle nodded. He didn't look up from his work.

"Jack Capehart owns a Kentucky racer. Does he board it here?"

"Yes. That black-leg bay yonder."

"Would you know if he took it out late yesterday?"

"I would know. He did not."

Torn didn't want to offend, but he had to see for himself. "Mind if I take a look?"

The laconic Creek merely shrugged.

Torn gave the horse a quick but thorough once-over. Seeing such a fine-looking animal made him nostalgic. The stables at Ravenoak, the Torn plantation in South Carolina, had been filled with horses of this caliber. This train of thought taunted him with bittersweet recollections, and left him with an aftertaste of ashes. The Ravenoak thoroughbreds were gone, as was Ravenoak itself.

He failed to find what he was looking for—scratches on that sleek reddish-brown hide. Nellie Bond's murderer had taken his mount through some thick brush. A hard-run horse could be combed and curried to perfection, but scratches took time to heal. Capehart's bay had nary a mark on him.

Torn shrugged it off and retraced his steps to the front of the livery, admitting to himself that he was grasping at straws.

He and Doc Crane walked down the Texas Road together into the heart of North Fork Town, and for a couple of minutes no word passed between them. Torn spent the time debating whether to show Nellie Bond's letter to Crane, and in the end decided to do so. He took the letter out of his pocket and handed it to the doctor.

"I think you'll find this interesting," he said.

Crane frisked himself, found his spectacles, and hooked the see-betters over his ears. Then he scratched a match to life with his thumbnail. He read the letter. The match burned down. He lit another and read the letter a second time.

"God in heaven," he breathed. "Where did you get this? Was it on the body?"

"In her carpetbag. She dropped the bag as she was running for her life."

"Whoever she wrote this to is the murderer. If only she'd seen fit to address it. So that's what you meant when you told that crowd back there that the murderer made a mistake when he killed Katy O'Keefe."

"Right. It was Nellie Bond he was after. Somehow he knew the woman blackmailing him worked on Broken Wagon. It wasn't until after he killed Katy that he realized she wasn't the one."

"How would he find that out?"

"I don't know."

Crane's face was very pale in the darkness.

"But you found this letter, he didn't. Does he know he killed the right woman the second time around?"

"That's the big question. He won't be getting any more extortion letters. If he *is* finished, it'll be that much harder to catch him."

They walked for a spell before Crane spoke again.

"Why did you show this to me?"

Torn shrugged. "Thought someone else should know."

Crane peered at him. "In case something happens to you."

"Right."

Crane gave him the letter. "Good luck."

"Thanks. I'm going to need it."

At the intersection of the Texas Road and the California Trail they parted company, Crane heading for his office on the latter and Torn making for the jailhouse.

Inside the jailhouse, Torn groped through the darkness for the kerosene lamp on the desk. He got it lighted, then spun at a whisper of sound.

Trooper O'Malley was crouched in a corner of the room, a pistol aimed at Torn.

"Don't try it," growled the horse soldier.

Torn's Colt was halfway out of its holster.

"I don't want to kill you," said O'Malley.

Torn gauged his chances and saw they were nil. He breathed deeply and let the Colt slip back into the holster.

"Glad to hear it," he said.

"I've got a story you're going to want to hear."

Torn had a hunch he was about to get some answers.

CHAPTER 23

THE NEXT DAY, TORN AND O'MALLEY REACHED FORT
Gibson in the quickening twilight. Arriving from the south,
they crossed the Neosho River by means of the army ferry,
then followed a road up through thick woods to the outpost
built on a hill commanding the river.

Most of the fort's buildings—headquarters, stables, bar-
racks and hospital—were made of stone, and roofed with
slate, encircled by a picket stockade with blockhouses at
the corners. The Stars and Stripes hung limply from the
parade-ground flagpole. Not a breath of air stirred the
muggy heat of a summer evening.

Guards at the gate challenged them. Identifying himself,
Torn told the sentries he had come to see Colonel Finney,
the fort's commanding officer. One of the soldiers entered
the fort, carrying this information to the sergeant of the
guard. Torn waited patiently, while O'Malley had the look
of a rabbit ready to run. That he had managed to persuade

O'Malley to come this far amazed Torn.

When the sergeant of the guard proved to be Jurgen, O'Malley made a funny noise deep in his throat and tightened up on the reins. His horse began to fiddlefoot. Torn reached over and latched onto a bridle cheekstrap.

"Don't," he said curtly. "This is your only chance and you know it."

He watched the progress of the war between reason and fear in O'Malley's eyes.

"Arrest that trooper," snapped Jurgen, pointing at O'Malley, and the sentries took a step, Sharps carbines at the ready.

"No," said Torn, and the word cracked like a rawhide whip, stopping the sentries in their tracks.

"This man is wanted on a charge of desertion," growled Jurgen.

"He's in my custody."

"The hell he is."

"You lay a hand on my prisoner, Sergeant, and I'll take you down another notch."

Jurgen's beefy face darkened as he remembered the humiliation he had suffered at Torn's hands in North Fork Town. The sergeant proved to have more sense than Torn gave him credit for. He forced a cold smile and backed down.

"Trooper Caldwell will escort you to the colonel."

"Don't you want to come along, Sergeant?" asked Torn. "What O'Malley here has to say to the colonel might be of interest to you."

Jurgen glowered at O'Malley. The three-striper was worried. Torn knew he had every reason to be.

"Trooper Caldwell," rasped Jurgen.

"Yessir!" One of the sentries, a fuzzy-cheeked youngster, snapped to and addressed Torn. "If you'll follow me, sir..."

"Lead on."

As he rode stirrup-to-stirrup with Torn, following the trooper into the fort, O'Malley threw frequent, anxious looks over his shoulder.

"The bastard'll backshoot me if he gets half a chance," muttered O'Malley. "Just like he done Rutledge."

"It's too late," said Torn. "And he knows it."

As they crossed the parade ground, Torn took a long look around, wondering where Lieutenant Stride was, and deciding it wouldn't take long for Jurgen to deliver the bad news to Stride.

Torn did not see very many soldiers. For some time now, Fort Gibson had been manned by a skeleton crew. Most of the garrison was kept out in the field, patrolling the western border of the Creek Nation, chasing Kiowa and Comanche raiders. *An exercise in futility*, mused Torn, *if ever there was one.*

A single sentry at the door to the headquarters building came to brisk attention as Torn and O'Malley dismounted and handed their reins to Trooper Caldwell. The door flew open and Colonel Dolph Finney emerged.

Torn knew Finney from the colonel's days as commanding officer at Fort Smith. When that fort was closed, Finney had been transferred to Gibson. With twenty-five years of undistinguished service behind him, Finney was a temperamental, ascerbic career soldier who drank too much and paid as little attention to his duties as he could get away with, leaving the garrison's day-to-day operations to his subordinates.

"Evening, Colonel," said Torn. "I don't know if you remember me..."

"I know who you are." Finney peered bleary-eyed at

O'Malley. "I see you found our prodigal son. If you expect a hearty handshake, forget it."

"I'm not handing him over to you," said Torn.

"No? Why not?"

"Because he wouldn't survive the night in your guardhouse."

"What is that supposed to mean?"

"It means there are certain men in your command who would kill O'Malley before he could testify against them."

"What is going on here?" queried Finney, bewildered.

That, thought Torn, was the problem: Finney didn't have the slightest idea what had been happening right under his nose. Once robust, the colonel was now a man gone completely to seed. Puffy jowls bristled with a three-day stubble of beard. Bloodshot eyes and crosshatched veins on the tip of his nose were physical symptoms of his heavy reliance on alcohol. His white duck trousers and non-regulation fatigue blouse were soiled and wrinkled, his boots scuffed. He was not an officer who could lead by example.

"I think you ought to hear what O'Malley has to say," suggested Torn.

"Very well," sighed Finney, without much enthusiasm. "Come inside."

He slumped into a chair behind a desk cluttered with maps and reports, and adopted an attitude of determined indifference. He didn't invite them to sit down. O'Malley looked like he was too nervous to sit down anyway.

"So what is it I ought to hear?" asked Finney.

O'Malley gave Torn a sidelong look. Torn nodded.

"Rutledge was murdered, sir," announced O'Malley.

"He was shot while trying to escape. I have Lieutenant Stride's report right here in front of me." Finney rearranged the clutter. "Somewhere."

"No, sir. He was murdered."

"O'Malley, you've been out in the sun too long."

"I know what I'm talking about. Sir."

Finney snorted. "That's a matter of opinion. What is this? Some crazy scheme to exonerate yourself? It won't wash, mister. You deserted, and you stole army property to boot."

"That's what this is all about," said Torn. "Theft of army property. But we're not talking about horses."

"I wish I knew *what* we were talking about," complained Finney.

Torn planted his knuckles on Finney's desk and leaned forward.

"We're talking about the theft of guns and ammunition from the arsenal at Little Rock, Arkansas."

"When? How? Who?"

"I'll let O'Malley tell you. He was in on it. Along with Lt. Stride and Judge Ronan."

Finney blanched. "J. Carter Ronan?" he gasped.

Torn nodded grimly. "Worst part of it is that Big Mike Walker, the sheriff of North Fork Town, got wind of the scheme. He was killed before he could do anything about it."

"Who killed him?"

"That I don't know. Yet. But fair warning, Colonel—When I find out, and whether he's army or not, he's mine."

C H A P T E R

24

"IT ALL STARTED ABOUT A YEAR AGO," SAID O'MALLEY.
"At least for me and Rutledge and Sergeant Jurgen. One
day we were out on patrol and came across this wagon
full of crates, west of North Fork Town. We thought there
was something fishy about it, 'cause the California Trail was
real close by, and the driver was keeping clear of it. His
name was Creed Walker. The crates were supposed to
be full of farm implements, but there were guns, not shovels and such, in those crates."

"What kind of guns?" asked Finney.

"Spencer rifles, mostly. The kind the cavalry used in
the last year or two of the war. You know, the ones they
said you could load on Sunday and shoot the rest of the
week. 'Course, we got rifles now that carry more rounds,
but back then the Spencer was something to write home
about."

"Where did these weapons come from?"

"At first we didn't know. This Creed Walker, he wanted to fight, not talk. He would have made plenty trouble, too, except Sergeant Jurgen had the drop on him. Any time the sergeant's got a gun on you, you know you're a short hair away from meeting your Maker. Something about the sergeant..." O'Malley smiled ruefully. "You can just tell he'd like nothing better'n to blow a hole in you big enough to drive a Dougherty wagon through. But this Walker, when the sergeant started talking arrest, told us we'd do well to check with Lieutenant Stride first."

"He did, did he?"

"Yes, sir. And Walker had papers on him, saying he'd been hired to transport these so-called farm implements up to the Wichita Agency on the South Canadian."

"Hired by who?"

"The Osage Trading Company."

"In other words," said Torn, "J. Carter Ronan."

"Right," nodded O'Malley.

"So you checked with Lieutenant Stride," said Finney.

"The sergeant did. Turns out the lieutenant had been stationed at the Little Rock arsenal before getting transferred out here. That was when Mr. Ronan was a judge up in Fort Smith. One way or another they got together and decided to steal guns and ammunition out of the arsenal."

"I don't recall any reports of theft at the Little Rock arsenal while I commanded the garrison at Fort Smith."

"Of course not," said Torn. "Stride took care of that. There's probably a stack of empty crates in the arsenal. Since they came out with the Trapdoor Springfield, the army doesn't use the Spencer anymore, so nobody's bothered to check them."

Finney looked around like a man who has misplaced his

most prized possession. Torn figured he was hunting for a bottle of ninety-proof nerve medicine.

"So who gets the Spencers?" asked the colonel.

"Creed Walker's Kiowas," said Torn. "And their Comanche cousins, I suppose. You know, Colonel—the ones who have been running your soldiers ragged and playing hell with the Civilized Tribes."

Finney glared at O'Malley. "So Stride cut you in. You and Rutledge and Sergeant Jurgen."

"Yes, sir. Ronan gives the lieutenant his share every time a shipment is sold."

"Where does Ronan keep these guns?"

"I don't know that, Colonel."

"How much do you get, O'Malley?"

"About a hundred dollars a month."

"My God, there must be money in gun smuggling."

O'Malley nodded. "But I knew it wouldn't last forever. A sweet deal never does. Me and Rutledge fouled up first. You see, we were the ones who went into town and got caught. We just wanted to spend a little of that money we'd been stashing away."

Finney was one step ahead of O'Malley now. "You were afraid of what Stride might do to cover his tracks."

"Not the lieutenant, so much as Sergeant Jurgen. The man just plain scares me, I'll admit it. With us facing court-martials, Stride would worry we might spill the beans about the deal with Ronan, hoping we might get off light that way. And I guess he was right, 'cause here I am doing just that."

"So he killed Rutledge," said Torn. "O'Malley here was smart enough to make a run for it."

"Yeah," said O'Malley, chagrined. "I gone over the hill. Only I didn't go far."

"Why not?" asked Finney. "You could have made it to Mexico."

"I guess so. Problem is, I got to thinking. I always get into trouble when I start to think. Rutledge and me, we were partners. Only friend I ever had, now that I mention it. And I had a gut feeling Lieutenant Stride and Sergeant Jurgen would do exactly what they did. So I turned my horse around and went back to North Fork Town. Waited just outside town. Saw Lieutenant Stride and the sergeant ride in on the Texas Road."

"You were going to try to free Rutledge?"

"I thought about trying to break him out of that jailhouse." O'Malley glanced at Torn. "Then I thought I better not. When they left town with Rutledge. I trailed 'em, looking for a chance. I was still looking for one when I saw Rutledge start running. Sergeant Jurgen shot him down." O'Malley shook his head bitterly. "I let my partner down, Colonel. I ran out on him. It's hard to live with. I think that's why I went to Judge Torn here. I wanted to do something to get back at Lieutenant Stride and the sergeant for killing my friend."

Torn said, "My guess is, Stride convinced Rutledge they'd let him escape. Probably because a trooper named Murphy was present. I doubt Murphy was, or had ever been, part of this."

"He doesn't know anything," vouched O'Malley.

Finney looked from O'Malley to Torn and back again. Chair legs scraped the floor as he stood abruptly. He stalked to the window providing a view of the parade ground. He paced to the desk, glanced sharply at them, then returned to the window, hands clasped tightly behind his back.

"Who killed the sheriff, O'Malley?"

"I don't know, Colonel. Honest I don't. Like I told Judge

Torn here, a couple weeks ago Sergeant Jurgen warned us to stay clear of the sheriff, as he was sniffing around."

Finney was silent a moment. Finally, he said, "Private, are you willing to testify against Lieutenant Stride?"

"Like I told you before, Colonel," said Torn. "This man is in my custody. I wanted him to tell you the story because you needed to know why I'm going to arrest Stride."

"Lieutenant Stride is an officer in the . . ."

"Selling guns to hostile Indians is a federal crime," snapped Torn. "As is transporting guns for that purpose across state lines."

"I remind you that Mr. O'Malley is a deserter."

"I told him we'd work something out. We will, won't we, Colonel?"

Finney strode to the office door and called the sentry in.

"Inform Lieutenant Stride I wish to see him immediately. I think you'll find him in his quarters."

"Yes, sir."

The sentry gone, Finney returned to his desk. As he sat down he was wearing a smile of grim satisfaction.

"I never liked that supercilious son of a bitch."

"Stride?" asked Torn.

"Exactly. But I've got that spit-and-polish limey bastard now, by God. Strutting around like some damn field marshal. Always trying to show me up. Acting like he was the only professional in the garrison. Thinks he's a better soldier than me, does he? We'll see. Quoting Clausewitz and reading Frederick the Great. Devising absurdly complicated maneuvers for action against the hostiles. But for the loss of men it would have entailed, I'd liked to have seen Lieutenant Stride lead a Murat-style charge into a Kiowa deathtrap. How sad I will never have that pleasure."

Torn heard a single gunshot. It was far off and muffled,

but there was no mistaking the sound.

The puzzlement on Finney's unshaven features was quickly replaced by an expression of horror. He stormed out of the room. Torn and O'Malley followed. The sentry was running toward them. Blue-coated soldiers poured out of doorways all over the post.

The sentry pulled up and snapped into sloppy attention. He was white as a boiled shirt. Breathing hard, he tried to make his report by the book.

"I regret to inform the Colonel that Lieutenant Stride has . . . is . . . the lieutenant is indisposed. Permanently."

Finney looked like a child whose fun has been spoiled. "The bastard killed himself, didn't he?"

"Yes, sir. I knocked on the door. He told me to enter. As I stepped in he said something about dying like a Spartan. Then he put his revolver in his mouth and pulled the trigger."

"I'm surprised he didn't quote one of Napoleon's Maxims," said Finney with callous sarcasm. "You were spared that, at least."

"Sir?"

"Never mind. Find Sergeant Jurgen. I want him placed under arrest."

"I don't think you'll find him," said Torn. "I figure he warned Stride, and then dusted out."

Finney grunted. "Well, O'Malley, I guess you'll be safe here with us, after all."

They returned to the colonel's office. Finney could refrain no longer and broke out a bottle. Declining the offer of a drink, Torn waited calmly. Lighting their way with lanterns, details pounded by outside. It was full dark now. Torn was almost certain Jurgen had escaped.

When a trooper arrived to announce that, indeed, the sergeant was not to be found on the post, Finney cut loose a hair-raising string of epithets.

"Don't worry," said Torn. "He won't go far."

"What makes you so sure?"

"Because I know what kind of man he is. He won't turn his back on a grudge. And he's got a grudge against me."

"You think he'll come gunning for you?"

Torn smiled. "I'm counting on it."

CHAPTER

25

TORN RODE BACK TO NORTH FORK TOWN THAT NIGHT, pushing the horse he had hired from John Eagle as hard as he dared. He had a hunch Jurgen might try to warn Ronan, who was undoubtedly the kind of man who would reward the sergeant handsomely for such an effort.

Three questions were foremost in Torn's mind. Who had killed Big Mike Walker? Who had paid those two would-be assassins a hundred dollars each to gun him down? And assuming Ronan still had some stolen army weaponry stashed away, where was this cache? Torn figured he could get all the answers from J. Carter Ronan himself.

One more corner to turn, mused Torn as he rode hell-for-leather down the Texas Road, *and I'm on the home stretch*.

It was becoming clear; he no longer felt like a mouse in a maze. He realized that by sheer coincidence he had accompanied a shipment of guns all the way from Fort

141

Smith to North Fork Town. The irony did not escape him. The *Jezebel* had carried crates of Spencer carbines disguised as farm implements, and Ronan had been waiting at the landing to oversee their off-loading. *What a shock for Ronan*, thought Torn, *to see me get off that sand-river steamer*. But Ronan had done an admirable job of keeping his wits about him. So had Captain Gill, who was in all likelihood yet another member of this gun-smuggling ring. Torn wondered what would have happened had he discovered the guns during the trip upriver. Alone against Gill and his crew, he might have ended up at the bottom of the Arkansas.

A few miles from Fort Gibson his mount began to stumble. Torn slowed the horse by degrees, from gallop to canter to walk, and finally dismounted to lead the animal for a spell. Putting a short rein on his impatience, Torn walked the lathered horse for a quarter of a mile. Silver moonlight threw his attenuated shadow out in front of him.

Walking this road put him in mind of Nellie Bond. Her murder, and Katy O'Keefe's, remained a mystery. He could see no possible connection between them and the gunrunning conspiracy.

First things first. He would mete out justice to Ronan, Jurgen, and Creed Walker—and save some for the murderer of the two women.

Judging the horse sufficiently cooled down, he climbed back into the saddle and rode for North Fork Town.

It was not quite midnight when he arrived. The streets were empty. He rode straight to the stone jailhouse. It was dark and quiet; this time he went in with Colt drawn, not caring to be taken by surprise again. Satisfied that no ambush awaited him, he lighted the kerosene lamp on the desk and immediately saw the note.

I KNOW WHO KILLED BIG MIKE. COME SEE
ME AND I WILL TELL YOU ALL YOU WANT TO
KNOW. SPANISH RED

He stood there a full minute, staring at the note, his
mind racing. The first thought that crossed his mind was
that this could be a trap. Then, for the first time, it occurred
to him that Spanish Red might very well be involved. He
had seen her in the company of Creed Walker, and Creed
was definitely involved.

Maybe Creed had killed Big Mike Walker, his own half-
brother. Conjecture only, but a disturbing possibility.
Creed was the prime suspect in every crime that occurred
in these parts. Perhaps in trying to get some concrete
evidence against Creed, Big Mike had stumbled upon the
gunrunning operation. Without a doubt, Creed had all the
makings of a backshooter.

Moving to the gunrack, Torn took down the Fox scattergun. He pocketed a handful of extra double-ought shells.
Stepping out into the boardwalk shadows, he paused, not
quite certain of his next move.

His first instinct was to go straight for Ronan, but could
he ignore the fact that Ronan, by dent of his marriage to
a Creek woman, was a citizen of the Creek Nation? If he
adhered strictly to the letter of the law, Torn needed a
warrant from the tribal council before arresting Ronan, and
another before he hunted down Creed Walker.

It was out of respect for Long Walker that Torn hesitated in following this course of action. If his suspicions
were on the mark, Big Mike had been killed by someone
involved in the gun smuggling. That meant Creed was tied
into the murder of North Fork Town's sheriff, whether he
actually did the deed himself or not. Long was an intelligent

man—he would reach the same conclusion. Torn was loath to break the news to Long.

Another consideration forestalled him from seeking out the Creek elder. Doc Crane had said it best: Long did not expect Torn to play by the rules. Creek law was sometimes too slow, too fair, to be just.

Torn mulled it over and decided to go after Ronan, but he would look Spanish Red up first. If the note proved to be bait for an ambush, so be it. If not, then he might get information from Spanish Red that would prove to be another nail in Ronan's coffin.

His stride long and quick with purpose, Torn headed for Virgin Alley, the sawed-off shotgun cradled in his arm, his keen eyes probing the night shadows.

Turning onto Broken Wagon Road, he spotted a woman's silhouette in a shanty doorway. She was wearing a frowzy, peach-colored wrapper and smoking a cigar. Heavy paint and powder did nothing to improve her looks. The mix of cheap perfume and perspiration was a rank bouquet he could not fail to notice as he drew near.

"Where can I find Spanish Red?"

She swayed flabby hips. "Won't I do, handsome?"

"Not the kind of trouble I'm looking for."

She dropped the salacious smile and nodded sideways. "Four doors down, mister."

He nodded thanks and moved on. The woman slipped inside her shanty and softly closed the door. Across the street was the shack once occupied by Katy O'Keefe, now dark and dismal. He spared it a grim glance; what he had seen there was still too vivid in his mind.

Tonight, Virgin Alley was dormant. Torn figured the murders had something to do with it. Further up the road he saw two other women lounging outside their shacks. They saw him, too—saw the shotgun and the way he moved—and as he watched they disappeared into their dens, as prudent as deer vanishing into brush at the first hint of danger.

A man burst out of Spanish Red's shack.

Torn was a half-dozen strides away. The man was a burly, bearded character wearing a sailor's cap and dungarees—Torn saw him clearly in light cast by a lantern hanging on a nail beside the door. The man took one look at Torn and bolted into an alley between the shanties.

Torn ran after him, reaching the mouth of the alley in time to see the man disappear behind Spanish Red's shack. Torn loped down the alley and took the corner with caution. He was wise to do so—the man was waiting for him. Moonlight gleamed on a knife's blade. Ducking under a vicious swipe, Torn drove the barrels of the Fox 10-gauge into the man's midsection, then brought the stock up into a face twisting with pain. The man landed flat on his back, then started to get up. Stepping on the hand holding the knife, Torn pressed the scattergun against the man's chest and thumbed back both hammers.

"Move and I'll send you straight to hell," he rasped.

No sound warned Torn, but the eyes of the man on the ground did. They flicked to something—or someone—in the alley. Torn's reflexes were lightning-fast, but this time they weren't fast enough. He was only beginning to turn when the blow to the back of his head sent him plummeting into black nothing.

CHAPTER 26

WHEN TORN CAME TO HE WAS LYING ON A FLOOR, AND the first thing he saw was a lot of blood on the scarred planking.

For a moment he thought it was his own blood, but soon realized that his only injury was a knot on the back of his head. It hurt like hell and his head was pounding. As he pushed up on hands and knees, groaning, funny white lights danced across his vision. His stomach rolled and he tasted bile. The world began to turn and tilt precariously. He fought against blackout.

Slowly raising his head, he looked around, wondering where he was. A small one-room shack. A kerosene lamp burned on a small table. Its light reflected off glistening swipes of blood on the walls.

"Christ," he muttered.

She lay on the floor, with one leg still up on the bed. A blood-slick sheet covered her from the waist up. He crawled over and pulled the sheet off her face. He didn't want to—it was the last thing he wanted to see—but he had to know her identity.

Spanish Red.

He could see the terrible open wound in her throat. Her head was tilted back, mouth open in a silent scream, and her dark eyes stared at him in dead surprise.

Drawing the sheet off her body he noticed she hadn't been cut open like Katy O'Keefe and Nellie Bond. So in a way it wasn't as bad. In another way it was worse.

Because his saber-knife had been buried to the hilt right between her breasts.

She hadn't been dead long. Blood still poured from the appalling gash in her throat. The warped planking of the floor sloped down toward the door. A small river of blood snaked across the floor and under the door, and he took a wild guess that Spanish Red had been murdered not ten minutes ago.

And he'd been framed.

It didn't take a genius to figure that out.

He felt for the Colt at his hip. The holster was empty. Grabbing the iron bedstead, he tried to get to his feet. The room tilted madly and began to spin. His hand slipped on blood and he fell to one knee.

Someone started pounding on the door.

"Hey! Who's in there? What's going on?"

A nice, neat job, thought Torn bitterly. He had no doubt Ronan was behind it. Somehow Ronan had found out Torn was hot on his trail; that Stride was dead by his own hand, O'Malley had spilled the beans, and Jurgen was on the run. Maybe Jurgen *had* warned him. Torn didn't know, and he wondered if he ever would, because this was a perfect frame. He could hear Ronan now, mentioning the fact that the Broken Wagon murders had started not long after Torn's arrival. As if anyone in this fear-gripped town would need reminding.

More than one person was shouting outside now. Two shots were fired. As they did not come through the door, Torn assumed they'd been sent skyward, designed to bring others to the scene. There was no way out for him except through that door or the draped window next to it. Should he run? That would be tantamount to an admission of guilt. But then what good would protestations of innocence do him in this predicament? It was dark outside; if he could break through the people gathered on the other side of that door he might have a slim chance of getting away.

And then what? He'd been a wanted man before— hunted like an animal after his killing of Schmidt and the escape from Point Lookout. He hadn't cared for it then and he didn't particularly want to give it a second try.

He hesitated, wasting precious seconds, and then it was too late. The door splintered at the latch and cracked back on its hinges. Part of Torn's mind—the part remaining coldly analytical—put this door-breaking down to foolish dramatics. The door was latched, not locked; it could be opened from the outside.

The first one through was a young man with a sunburnt face and dusty range clothes; a cowboy. Torn had never seen him before. Several other men surged in behind him, but the cowboy took one step into the shanty and stopped. Those in his wake jostled him, but he would not budge. His eyes got wide as saucers as he saw the body, the blood, Torn. The six-gun in his hand came up to point at Torn's chest. The cowboy was squeezing the hogleg so tightly his knuckles were white.

Torn held his hands out away from his sides.

"Take it easy with that charcoal-burner," he advised.

There followed a moment suspended in time, when no one spoke or moved or scarcely breathed.

Torn had figured the first man through the door would be, if not Ronan himself, then one of Ronan's hirelings. After all, they'd gone to a lot of trouble to frame him, and it was best for them if he were caught red-handed. Now Torn revised his thinking on that score. This cowboy had not been rehearsed. It was just his bad luck to be the first to see the blood leaking out under the door. He hadn't been prepared for the carnage that confronted him. The sight had shaken him badly, and he was as close to shooting as a man could get without actually doing the deed.

"Sweet Jesus!" gasped one of the men behind the range rider. "It's Spanish Red!"

"Lord have mercy, look at that . . ."

"I'm going to be sick . . ."

"He did it! Clay Torn's the one!"

"Reach for the rafters," bleated the cowboy.

"I'm unarmed," said Torn, fiercely calm.

"Just keep your damn hands up!" yelled the cowboy.

Torn heard running in the street. Moth-eaten velveteen drapes covered the window, but he didn't need to see the mob to know it was forming.

The men he could see, those filling the doorway, were getting over the initial shock. Their grim silence, the narrow and glittering way they looked at him, did not bode well.

"He killed Spanish Red!" shrilled a woman in the street.

Angry voices swelled into a thunderclap of outrage.

"I say hang him!"

"Get a rope!"

"Exalt the butcher!"

They had a case of lynch fever. Most of these men were respectable members of the community, and here they were, mingling with sporting ladies, many of whom were half-clad, and all joined together in common cause—all of them out for his blood. It didn't come as a shock to him. The mood of the crowd that had gathered when he and Windy and Doc Crane had brought Nellie Bond's body back to town had forewarned him. The community was worked up to fever pitch, and in the heat of the moment forgot the old prejudices. Here were respectable townsmen— men who yesterday would have shunned Spanish Red because of her profession—now clamoring to lynch the man they thought responsible for her murder.

"Get him!"

All it needed was the saying. As one, the men in the doorway surged forward—all but the firmly rooted cowboy, who was almost knocked down by the onslaught. They grabbed for Torn. He struck back, the instinct for self-preservation taking complete command. A half-dozen foes swarmed over him. One jabbed an elbow in his ribs. Another's fist grazed his jaw. Blows began to fall like rain. His own fist connected solidly with a man's jaw. The man went down and took another with him.

The charge drove Torn backward, slamming him into the wall. They tried to kick his legs out from under him; he strove to stay standing. Someone punched him in the throat. Torn's head bounced off the wall. He almost blacked out, pitching forward. Another vicious blow to the side of the head hammered him to the floor. Hands grabbed him roughly and dragged him across the shanty, out into the street. He wrestled free. They lost their grip on him and he hit the hardpack. As he pushed up, a man kicked him in the shoulder. He rolled into another kick, this one in the small of the back. That boiled his water. An almost diabolical fury, cold as saber steel, gave him new strength. He wrenched one man's legs out from under him, swarmed over his victim, pounding blow after blow into a face that quickly became covered with blood.

Someone whacked him on the back of the shoulder with the barrel of a sidegun. Torn figured the man was aiming for his skull, and he didn't give the bastard a second chance. He rolled into the man's legs, bringing him down, grabbed for the gun, and wrenched it free. In the blink of an eye he was on his feet and lunging at another man. This unfortunate was unarmed. Torn collared him in a chokehold and pressed the gun to his head.

The crowd took a collective step forward—and froze as he cocked the pistol.

"Another step," growled Torn, "and this town will be short one citizen."

He was the only one present who knew it was an empty threat.

He didn't give them time to reconsider, but began to back up, dragging his hostage along. Reaching the mouth of the alley, he gave the man a hard shove, spun on his heel, and ran for his life.

A couple of bullets chased him through the darkness, but he made it around the corner of Spanish Red's shanty unscathed, and paused to fire two rounds well over the heads of his pursuers. A quick over-shoulder glance revealed a vacant lot behind him, and on the other side the backs of buildings facing the Texas Road. He was across the lot and churning up another alley before the first pursuer emerged from the row of Virgin Alley shacks.

Torn burst onto the Texas Road and pulled up short.

Whispering Jack Capehart, on his thoroughbred bay, was galloping down the road from the north—the direction of John Eagle's livery. Hoke, also mounted, was following him. The black man was leading a third cayuse.

Capehart checked his Kentucky pure-blood so sharply

that the horse almost sat down in the middle of the street. He pulled the Dance revolver out of his red sash, and for a split second Torn thought he and Whispering Jack were about to trade hot lead. But Capehart sent his bullet past Torn and into the dirt at the feet of the mob just now spilling out of the alley.

This literally brought things to a standstill.

"Can you ride?" asked Capehart, glittering eyes taking in Torn's bloody, disheveled appearance.

Torn nodded curtly.

"Then I suggest you climb that horse Hoke is dragging."

"What are you doing, Capehart?" challenged an irate member of the lynch mob.

"Is that you, Draper?" Capehart smiled pleasantly. "I'll tell you what I'm *about* to do. I'm about to turn your wife into a widow."

This comment elicited belligerent murmurs from the crowd that clogged the mouth of the alley like a cork in a bottle, but no one made a threatening move. The Dance revolver and Whispering Jack's reputation gave all of them second thoughts. Torn, sore and winded, pulled himself into the saddle of the extra horse, and Hoke surrendered the reins.

"John Law," grinned Hoke, "you look like you'd have to get better to die. Kinda like the poor fools what got in the ring with me."

"He murdered Spanish Red!" someone howled, indignant. "Those other women, too!"

"You're helping a cold-blooded killer escape, Capehart!" chimed in another.

"This man was framed," replied Whispering Jack, as casually as if he were commenting on the weather. He backed the thoroughbred up until he was alongside Torn and Hoke. "Dust out!" he yelled, wheeling the horse around and kicking it into a gallop. Torn and Hoke followed suit. A few parting shots were fired by the mob, but they were quickly out of range.

A mile out of North Fork Town they pulled up to give their mounts a breather. Torn checked their backtrail, listening for the sound of pursuit. Nothing. The moon had left the sky, and he was relieved to know that dawn would not be long in coming.

It had been one hell of a long night.

CHAPTER

27

ONCE THEY WERE CONFIDENT THERE WOULD BE NO PUR-
suit, they turned off the Texas Road, plunging into the
brush in a northwesterly direction. Whispering Jack took
the lead, and Torn wanted to know where Capehart was
going, but he held his tongue until they dropped single-file
into a willow-choked hollow where a sweetwater spring
seeped from a limestone ledge.

They dismounted and let their horses drink. Dawn was
beginning to pearl the eastern rim of the sky, and betrayed
stormclouds gathering to the south under cover of the fast-
fading night. Capehart found a rock to sit on, lighted a
claro cigar, and seemed quite content to watch and listen
to wrens flitting through the bright green branches of the
trees. Hoke hunkered down by the spring and watched
the horses, grinning, talking to them, telling them not to
drink too much as they had miles to go before they slept,
scolding them gently the way a parent would his children.

It was one of life's contradictions, mused Torn, *that a man like Hoke, so gentle and guileless, had once made a living by pounding other men into bloody pulp.*

Torn did not feel at ease with either of these men, for he did not know their motives. And he wasn't used to being unarmed. He had no idea where the Fox scattergun or his Colt Peacemaker were at this moment. His saber-knife when last seen, had been buried to the hilt in Spanish Red. He checked his pockets, found that he still possessed the extra shotgun shells and, most importantly, the photograph of Melony Hancock. But that was about it.

"I want some answers," he told Capehart.

"Fire away."

"Where are we going?"

"That woman's place."

"What woman?"

"You know. The one you took to that shivaree down at the council house the other night."

"Angevine? You know a lot."

"I keep my eyes and ears open."

"Why her place?"

"You have anywhere else you can go?"

"Back to North Fork Town."

Capehart chuckled. "You don't want to do that."

"What I don't want to be is on the run," replied Torn, cold-eyed. "I've had that experience once before, and once was enough. Besides, I don't want Ronan to get away."

"He won't," said Capehart, fiercely. "No matter how far or fast he runs. And he will. Run, I mean. You see, you aren't supposed to be alive. He figured they'd hang you, and he'd get away with murder."

"You're saying Ronan murdered those women?"

"He's responsible. I thought you knew."

"I'm after him because he's selling guns to the Kiowas

and Comanches through Creed Walker. You seem to know a lot about what's going on. Why didn't you tell me sooner?"

Capehart let smoke trickle through his teeth while he contemplated the inch of gray ash on the end of his expensive cigar.

"I thought you and Ronan were friends."

"We were never friends," said Torn. "I admit, I felt I owed him. And I respected him. I thought he stood for law and order."

Capehart's laugh was bitter.

"How much do you know?" pressed Torn.

"It all revolves, in a way, around Spanish Red. You see, Ronan would bring in a shipment of guns. His men would move them out to some isolated spot in the hills. When Creed Walker brought the payment to Spanish Red, Ronan would tell her where the shipment was hidden. It was a different place every time. Ronan would get the payment through Spanish Red, and Creed Walker would find out where the guns were through her, too. You might say she was the go-between. As you might imagine, Creed and Ronan don't trust each other. Can't say that I blame either one of them."

"Where did Creed get the money to pay for the guns?"

"Most Creek and Cherokee farmers keep their money in a jar under the floor, or behind a stone in the fireplace. They don't care to put their hard-earned life savings in the banks around here, with good reason. It would go straight into the pockets of the hundred or so bank robbers currently operating in the Nations. And how many emigrants head west without a grubstake?"

"So they hit the wagon trains and the farms and use the money they find to buy Ronan's guns."

Capehart nodded. "That's the only way I can figure it. Pretty soon, every Kiowa and Comanche warrior will be armed with a Spencer carbine and plenty of ammunition. Then, God help the Nations."

It literally set Torn's teeth on edge. J. Carter Ronan was selling guns to the enemies of the Five Civilized Tribes and that was bad enough, but what really angered Torn was Ronan's accepting as payment for those guns money taken from good folks murdered by his savage clients.

"How did you find out about it?" he asked Whispering Jack.

Capehart's features took on a solemn cast. He flicked the half-smoked claro away, anger in the gesture.

"Katy O'Keefe."

"How did she know?"

"From Spanish Red. A few months ago, Spanish Red came down with a fever. She was violently ill. Katy took care of her. At first, Spanish Red thought she'd been poisoned, and she thought Ronan had done it. She came to realize that her situation was, shall we say, precarious. She knew too much, and she was afraid Ronan might come to the same conclusion. You know the old saying. No honor among thieves. No one knows that better than a thief.

"She took a liking to Katy. She was surprised that Katy would go to so much trouble caring for her while she was sick. Women like Spanish Red don't expect to be treated nicely. It had a strong effect. But that's the kind of person Katy was."

"So she told Katy all about it?"

"Better than that. She put it all down in writing. Then she asked Katy to keep this deposition in a safe place, and to turn it over to Big Mike or the lighthorse if anything happened to her. She trusted Katy. There was something about Katy you could trust."

"But Katy told you."

"Not until later. Not until the deposition came up missing. Katy panicked. She came to me with the whole story. She suspected Nellie Bond of stealing Spanish Red's confession, and she was afraid of what Nellie might try to do with the information."

"She tried to blackmail Ronan."

Capehart stood and paced, suddenly restless. His eyes were bright and hard. "Yes, and she got Katy killed in the bargain."

Torn watched him for a moment, reading the man.

"I found a lock of your hair in Katy O'Keefe's place."

Capehart stopped pacing. He stood with his back to Torn, his head tilted back slightly, and Torn assumed he was looking up at the quickly-fading stars.

"To hell with it," he muttered.

"You cared for her, didn't you."

"About her."

Say goodbye to her for me.

"Sorry," said Torn.

"She was on the wrong side of thirty, but she seemed to me like a little girl lost, searching for something, someone, to cling to. I never could get her to talk about her past, but I firmly believe hers was a good life at first. Somewhere along the way it took a turn for the worse. Despite all she'd been through, she still managed to care for others. I suppose she was so accustomed to rough handling that the smallest kindness meant more to her than perhaps it should have. When I told her I could no longer come calling, she wept. Asked for a lock of hair to remember me by. She had a notion that I was vain about my hair." Capehart turned, wearing a sad half-smile. "Hickok—now *he's* vain. But me? Nonetheless, I obliged her."

"Was it you I almost shot the night Katy was killed?"

"Nossuh," said Hoke, and Torn whirled to find the black

goliath standing right behind him. "It was me."

Torn was astonished that a man so big could move so light on his feet. Hoke was watching Capehart, and his scarred brow was furrowed with deep concern., For whatever reason, he was intensely loyal to Whispering Jack.

"I sent him," said Capehart. "I'd made up my mind that it would be best for Katy if she left North Fork Town. I gave Hoke two hundred dollars and told him to take it to her."

"I gave her the money," said Hoke. "I left her place, and was down the street a ways when I seen an army man go up to her door. Didn't think nothin' of it—didn't know at the time what was goin' on—so I kept walkin'. Then I hears the scream. It spooked me plenty. I started runnin'."

"So you see," said Whispering Jack, "you did almost shoot an innocent man."

"The man I saw was wearing a cloak or coat."

Hoke nodded. "Yassuh. That was Mr. Jack's coat."

"Poor Hoke," smiled Capehart. "He didn't want to be recognized."

Hoke nodded vigorously. "That's right. It don't sit well with folks when they sees a black man payin' attention to a white woman. Even a sportin' lady like thems that live on Broken Wagon."

"Hoke had a bad experience," remarked Capehart.

"I didn't do nothin', that time back in New Orleans. But when people make up their minds they seen something, there ain't no unmakin' it, most times."

"One of my coats was hanging in Pete Shagrue's storeroom," explained Capehart. "I let Hoke wear it that night."

"And it's made of blue pilot-cloth," said Torn.

"As a matter of fact, it is."

Turning back to Hoke, Torn said, "You mentioned an army man. Did you get a good look at him?"

"Yassuh. He didn't see me, though. A big man. Had stripes on his shirt. Bald, too. Seen that when he took his cap off, as he was going inside Miss Katy's place."

"Jurgen," said Torn.

"You know him?" asked Capehart.

"We've met. A sergeant out of Fort Gibson. He and a Lieutenant Stride were in on the gun smuggling. Stride's dead."

Capehart slowly drew the Bowie knife from his red cummerbund. At that moment the sun peeked over the wooded hills to the east, and the Bowie's blade gleamed with the first light of day.

"So is this Jurgen," whispered Capehart. "Spanish Red didn't say anything about the army, so Katy must have thought he was just another customer. Well, I'm going to cut him up just like he did Katy."

"I don't blame you for feeling the way you do," said Torn. "And I suppose there's a certain kind of justice in it."

"Yes," said Whispering Jack. "Steel justice."

CHAPTER 28

MUCH AS HE HATED TO, TORN DECIDED TO SWALLOW his pride and not go storming back into North Fork Town. He had a hunch the citizens weren't likely to give him time to tell his side of the story. And if they lynched him, Ronan won. That would be hard to live with. Or, more precisely, hard to die with.

It all made sense to him now. The gun smuggling and the Broken Wagon murders were connected, after all. But what solid evidence did he have? Trooper O'Malley's story—and how many would believe a deserter, a man involved by his own admission in a criminal enterprise?

Now the question was: what would Ronan do? Would he sit tight and try to bluff his way through, or would he run? He had to be worried that Torn was on the loose. Torn realized that his reputation for dealing out swift justice—the rules of evidence be damned—had to be making Ronan extremely nervous at this very moment. Ronan had to be wondering if Torn would get to him before the vigilantes of North Fork Town got to Torn.

Problem was, it wasn't enough to go gunning for Ronan, secure in his own mind that the ex-judge-turned-gunrunner was due a comeuppance. *The fact remains*, mused Torn, *that I'm wanted for the Broken Wagon murders*. Somehow he had to prove he'd been framed by Ronan. He needed a plan.

So he decided to ride on to Angevine's.

That course of action was not entirely free of risk. Capehart had assumed there was a relationship between him and Angevine. Might not others come to the same conclusion?

Leaving the hidden spring, they rode north and west, eventually arriving at the California Trail. From a brush-covered bluff they watched the emigrant road for a half-hour, and in that time spotted only a solitary wagon. A man and a woman up front, a young girl dangling sunburned legs off the tailgate, an older boy hazing a laggardly milk cow with a long switch. Torn hoped they would make it past the Kiowas and Comanches, so well-armed thanks to J. Carter Ronan.

Though they saw no sign of a posse, they stayed off the trail, traveling parallel to it. Thunderclouds blocked the morning sun. Jagged lightning to the south was accompanied by growling thunder.

"We be in for a real frog-strangler," predicted Hoke, apprehensive of the approaching storm.

They reached Angevine's cabin before it rained. She saw them coming out of a gray gloom that had gathered in the grove of oaks and sycamores, and stepped out onto the porch with an old Hawken single-shot in her grasp—a long gun that had once belonged to her fur-trapper father. When they got closer she recognized Torn, and gasped at the blood and bruises on his face. Resting the Hawken against the cabin wall, she ran to him and walked alongside his horse, her hand on his leg. Dismounting, Torn discovered just how stiff and sore he was.

"What happened?" she cried. "Who did this to you?"

"About half the population of North Fork Town," said Torn wryly.

Capehart turned to Hoke. "Try to hide the horses, Hoke, but not too far from the cabin."

Hoke nodded, led the mounts around the corner of the cabin and out of sight.

"I'll make some coffee," said Angevine, and went inside.

Torn slacked into a rocking chair on the porch. "Why did you do it, Jack?"

"What?"

"Throw in with me."

"I'd like to see Ronan brought down hard."

"That's the only reason?"

"There's another. I don't ever want to see an innocent man die for a crime he didn't commit. And I especially can't abide lynch mobs. I was almost hanged by one myself."

"When was this?"

"Many years and miles ago. Up in Colorado Territory; I was on my way to a goldfield. A mob jumped me. Well, they called themselves a posse. They'd been on the trail of a tinhorn bottom-dealer who'd killed a miner and made off with the man's poke. They mistook me for that tinhorn and decided to string me up. They had the noose around my neck and the rope over a convenient tree limb when two more men rode up. One was the dead miner's partner. He allowed that I didn't really look like the man he'd seen running from the claim. He was the only one, apparently, who got a look at the killer. The others realized their mistake and cut me loose. They'd seen my clothes and my California prayer book, and just got it into their heads they were going to treat me to a necktie social. Had that miner been a half-minute later showing up, my bones would be decorating a Colorado mountainside."

"So that's why you do your level best to keep men off the gallows."

"Let me tell you something about Ronan. He's a cold-blooded son of a bitch. He didn't much care if a man was guilty or not. He just liked to see them swing. Same as that goldfield posse; they just had the urge to hang somebody that day, whether it was the right man or not."

"And you enjoyed robbing Ronan of his pleasure," said Torn. "Regardless of whether in doing so you helped a guilty man go free."

Capehart gave him a hostile look, and without another word went inside.

The wind kicked up, thrashing the trees, and a moment later the rain began to fall, gently at first. Angevine came out with a bowl of hot water and a cloth and began to clean the cuts and scrapes on Torn's face. She looked worried, but asked no questions. He smiled reassuringly and volunteered no information, keeping his thoughts to himself.

He decided Capehart was right about Ronan—the man was a cold-blooded son-of-a-bitch. *He played me for a fool*, thought Torn. Making sure Torn saw him on Broken Wagon the night of Katy's murder was a finesse move. Would someone involved in murder be so obvious? From the first, Torn had scratched him from the list of suspects.

Ronan's performance later that same night in the jailhouse had been brilliant, convincing Torn that his motives for being in Virgin Alley were painfully personal.

It made sense that Ronan had employed the sergeant to do his dirty work for him. For one thing, Ronan obviously didn't have the stomach for it. Secondly, Katy had had no reason to suspect Jurgen. Spanish Red hadn't known about the army connection to the gun smuggling conspiracy, so Katy couldn't have known, either. Ronan had no doubt made it plain to Stride and Jurgen that if he was incriminated as a result of Spanish Red's letter, they would be too. Knowing the kind of man Jurgen was, Torn figured the sergeant had probably volunteered for the duty.

Ronan had first assumed it was Spanish Red who'd been blackmailing him. She had admitted having Katy put everything down in writing. Trying to save her own life, Katy must have shared with Jurgen her suspicion that Nellie Bond had stolen the letter. Jurgen had killed her, anyway.

Running for her life, Nellie hadn't waited around for a stage or train, assuming she could hitch a ride on the well-traveled Texas Road, but Jurgen had found her first.

By this time, however, Ronan had decided Spanish Red was a liability. Jurgen had warned him that O'Malley had talked, Stride had killed himself, and Torn was hot on their trail. So Ronan had killed two birds with one stone, framing Torn and disposing of Spanish Red.

Torn could envision Ronan persuading Spanish Red that her indiscretions would be forgiven if she wrote the letter luring Torn into ambush. Cold-blooded, indeed.

Capehart stepped out of the cabin.

"Hoke's not back yet?"

Torn shook his head.

"He's probably talking to those horses again." Whispering Jack watched the rain for a moment, then said, "Got any ideas about what to do?"

"One. I'm going to get word to Long that I'm coming in."

"You're crazy."

"Long will hear me out. I'll tell him everything I know."

"Where's the proof?"

"I'm betting Ronan won't wait to find out if I have any. He went to a lot of trouble to frame me for murder. Maybe I don't have any real proof, but he doesn't know that. Desperate men do desperate things. I'm betting he'll try to stop me from getting to Long."

Capehart took a deep breath, let it out slow, and shook his head dubiously. "I don't think that dog will hunt."

"I'll go to Long," and Angevine.

Both men stared at her.

"No," said Torn.

"I don't know exactly what's happened," she said, "but obviously both of you would be risking your lives if you went anywhere near North Fork Town. I'll go. No one will bother me."

"She has a point," admitted Whispering Jack.

"I don't like it," said Torn.

"She'd be safer if she goes," said Capehart. "I reckon there's a posse out looking for us. Sure, they probably figure we're halfway to Texas by now, but somebody might get the bright idea to look for us here."

"All right," conceded Torn. "But you can at least wait until the storm passes."

"A little rain never hurt anybody," she replied, and disappeared into the cabin, giving him no chance to protest.

"She'll need a fast horse," said Capehart. "She can take my thoroughbred."

Torn stood, suddenly restless. "I'll fetch it."

The rain was really coming down now. Lightning crackled, followed by a peal of thunder louder than an entire battery of sixteen-pounders fired at once.

"I won't try to stop you," said Capehart wryly.

Torn picked up the Hawken and left the shelter of the porch. Sloshing across sodden ground, he was soaked clear through in less than a minute. The rain descended in sheets. Water poured off his drooping hat brim. He headed for the river, where the trees were thicker.

Where was Hoke? He remembered how the approaching storm had made Hoke nervous. Would he willingly stay out in such a storm?

Something rustled the brush to his left; he whirled, crouching, the Hawken held at hip level. One shot, he reminded himself. Better make it count.

But he didn't have to shoot. Hoke's horse appeared, dragging rein, gave him a long look, then wandered off, head bowed in the deluge.

The horse running loose convinced Torn that something was wrong. He moved on, deafened by the long drumrolls of thunder, half-blinded by the rain and the frequent flashes of lightning.

Then he saw Hoke.

The black man was sitting with his back to a tree trunk, legs splayed, chin resting on his chest.

When he got closer, Torn could see that Hoke's throat had been cut.

CHAPTER 29

TORN SAT ON HIS HEELS IN FRONT OF THE DEAD MAN, hit harder than he had expected to be. He didn't like to see good men die—there weren't enough good men to spare.

A guttural Kiowa war cry preceded the sharp, flat percussion of the gunshot. It was all the warning Torn needed. He lunged to one side, and the bullet kicked up a geyser of mud where he had been hunkered down a heartbeat earlier.

Creed Walker, bent low in the saddle of a galloping horse, was bearing down on him. The barrel of his sidegun spat flame twice more. One bullet winged close enough for Torn to hear. He didn't scramble for cover. He'd been shot at too many times to lose his nerve. The key to survival, he knew, was to bring down the man trying to kill you before he succeeded. He also knew that a man on a hard-running horse needed a lot of luck to hit what he was aiming at.

Torn brought the Hawken's stock to shoulder. Creed veered the horse off its dead-on course. One leg hooked around the cantle of his saddle, clinging to the pommel with one hand, he slid down out of sight on the far side of his mount and fired another shot at Torn from beneath the animal's neck. An old Plains Indian trick, providing the enemy with nothing to shoot at.

Cursing softly, Torn wondered if Creed was giving up and making a break for the tall timber. It was the old hit-and-run technique Torn had used quite often as a cavalry commander in the war. Go in fast, do what damage you can, then dust out before the enemy's resistance stiffened. Or maybe Creed was just planning to swing around and come at him from a different direction. Torn didn't know, and he wasn't going to wait and find out. There was no way he could let Creed Walker escape.

So he spent his one bullet and shot Creed's horse.

Torn's shot killed the animal instantly; the horse nose-dived, and Creed was thrown twenty feet. Breaking into a run, Torn tried to reach Creed before he could get to his feet, but Creed was resilient—the fall hadn't fazed him and he hadn't lost his grip on the pistol. Torn was still twenty feet shy of the mark when Creed stood up.

Torn had both hands on the barrel of the Hawkens now, intending to use the empty rifle like a club if he got close enough to do so. But now it didn't look as though he would live long enough to get that close. He hurled the Hawken. Creed made the mistake of trying to dodge and shoot at the same time. The bullet went wide and the rifle struck him squarely in the chest. He lost his footing in the mud and went down. Before he could get up a second time, Torn was on him.

They grappled, rolled, fighting for the pistol wedged between them. Torn got a hand on the barrel and twisted. The gun went off, a muffled report. He didn't know at first if he'd been hit or not, and drove a fist into Creed's snarling face. Walker shook loose and got up, staggering. Torn lunged. Creed tried to crack his skull with the empty pistol, but Torn slipped under and hit him squarely in the chest. Creed went down and took Torn with him. They went sliding through the mud.

Creed kept trying to pistol-whip Torn. The gunbarrel grazed Torn's head. He grabbed the gun and tried to wrench it out of Creed's grasp. Creed hammered him in the side with a knee, knocking Torn away. Torn rolled onto his back, kicked into Creed's charging form, and sent Walker sprawling.

Creed had lost the empty gun, but he still had a knife in his belt, and as he gained his feet he drew the blade. Torn dropped into a crouch. They began to circle beneath the wind-whipped trees, two men covered with mud, pelted by the relentless rain.

"You killed Spanish Red," snarled Creed. "Now I'm going to kill you."

He lunged, savagely swinging the knife. Torn blocked with a downswept arm and hooked Walker with a punishing left. Creed fell to one knee. Torn kicked the knife out of his hand. Creed tackled him around the knees. Clawing for the knife, Torn found it lay just inches beyond his fingertips. Creed tried to roll him over. Torn's heel caught him under the chin. Mud covered them both, and Creed lost his grip on Torn's legs. Kicking free, Torn grabbed the knife, rolled, and came up into Creed's charge.

The blade grated against Creed's ribs, then slipped in to the hilt. Creed's body went rigid as the knife pierced his heart. Torn stepped aside and let him pitch forward on his face.

Heading back for Hoke's body, Torn saw Whispering Jack running through the trees, Dance revolver in hand.

"What happened?" asked Capehart.

"Hoke's dead," said Torn dully, and walked on.

Whispering Jack followed him. They stood a moment in the rain, over the body. Not a word passed between them as they carried Hoke to the cabin and laid him out in the shelter of the porch.

Torn slumped into the rocking chair, sore from head to heels. His scrape with the mob and the fight-to-the-death with Creed had severely tested his endurance.

Angevine came out of the cabin with a blanket. Capehart took it from her and covered Hoke. He took one last, long look at the dead man's face.

"I guess you killed the man who did this," muttered Whispering Jack.

"I did. It was Creed Walker."

"Creed!" gasped Angevine. "Why did he come here?"

"Looking for me," replied Torn. "For revenge. He saw us together at the council house, remember?"

"Hoke was a good man," said Capehart. "One more debt Ronan owes."

Torn was glad now that they had come to Angevine's. He shuddered to think what might have happened to her had she been alone when Creed came calling.

CHAPTER

30

GOING BACK INTO THE WOODS TO CATCH THE HORSES, Torn passed Creed's dead mount. The rain was beginning to let up now. He slid Creed's rifle out of the saddle scabbard; it was a Spencer carbine. Torn recalled Doc Crane saying that Big Mike Walker had been killed with a gun that was .50 caliber or better. The Spencer carbine took a .56–50 bottleneck cartridge. Torn was sure this was the gun used in the killing of North Fork Town's sheriff.

He found a box of the .56 bottleneck in the saddlebags. And something else—a Colt single action army model. The initials MW were carved into the pistol's yellow bone grips.

It had to be Big Mike's gun.

Big Mike had been ambushed, shot in the back. That was right up Creed's alley. Creed had murdered his own half-brother and kept Mike's gun as a souvenir. Torn decided killing Creed Walker was his good deed for the day. His only regret was the grief this would bring Long.

Carrying the Spencer, with Big Mike's Colt in his holster, he walked down to the river and, as he expected, found two of the horses, including Capehart's Kentucky racer. On his way back to the cabin, the third horse, Hoke's, fell in step behind.

Whispering Jack was sitting on the porch steps, puffing on a claro, wearing the unmistakable look of one who wishes to be left strictly alone. Torn didn't bother him. He tied the horses to one of the porch uprights and entered the cabin. It was a two-room affair bearing a woman's touch. Neat and clean, with curtains on the windows, a sampler on the wall, and a quilt on the feather bed in the second room.

Angevine sat at the table, her hands clasped tightly, her lips parted, giving her a look of breathlessness. He knew she was worried and confused and probably more than a little scared. He admired her courage. Sitting down across from her, he put his big, scarred hand over hers.

"It's going to be all right," he said.

She sighed, closed her eyes, nodded. "Do you still want me to go to Long?"

"I don't *want* you to, but . . ." He took Big Mike's pistol out of his holster and laid it on the table between them.

She blanched, seeing the initials. "Oh, God. Is that . . ."

"Yes. I found it in Creed's saddlebags. I hate asking you to do this, but I want you to take this gun with you. Give it to Long. Tell him I'm bringing Creed in, and this is the proof. Tell him Creed has information that will clear me and implicate Ronan."

A look of horror stole across her face. "But Creed's dead . . . Clay, you're asking me to lie to Long!"

He squeezed her hand. "If there was any other way, believe me, I wouldn't ask this of you."

"But why?"

"It's a long story. Ronan and Creed were in business together smuggling guns. Big Mike found out and Creed backshot him. Then I found out and Ronan framed me for the murder of Spanish Red, but Creed wasn't in on that. You see, in his own way, Creed had feelings for Spanish Red. He didn't know Ronan was responsible for her death. He came here to kill me because he thought I was. And Ronan didn't want him to think any different."

"How can you be sure?"

You killed Spanish Red. Now I'm going to kill you.

And Rutledge to Creed, in the council house fight: *Didn't know she was your own private stock.*

Torn nodded. "I'm sure."

"I don't understand any of this, Clay."

"Just trust me. One more thing. Tell Long to clear the streets. I want the word spread that I'm coming after Ronan."

She rose, took two steps toward the door, then turned back. Her expression told him that suddenly she understood.

And what she understood scared her.

"Clay, don't do this!"

She'd left the Colt pistol on the table. Torn took it to her. Instead of taking the gun she threw her arms around his neck and kissed him—a fierce, feverish kiss.

When she broke away he caught a brief glimpse of tear-glistening eyes. She took the gun and rushed out the door. A moment later he heard a horse galloping away.

He looked bleakly around the cabin. A faint, sweet aroma came to him. Angevine. *A man could do a lot worse,* he thought.

The idea of staying here, spending the rest of his life with Angevine, had strong appeal.

But he knew it wouldn't work. It wouldn't be fair to her.

There would always be another woman. A woman named Melony Hancock. Until he found Melony, his past would never leave him alone, and he would not be able to live for the future.

Bone-tired, he shuffled to the door of the second room and paused on the threshold, leaning heavily against the frame. The bed beckoned him. Then he imagined how her cherry-colored hair would look, tousled on the pillow. How her firm, slender body would feel pressed against his under the white coverlet with its edging of tiny, embroidered roses. Felt her warm breath against his skin, the sweet taste of her lips . . .

Bitter, he swung away and left the cabin in a hurry.

Capehart was on the porch steps, as before. His brooding exasperated Torn.

"If you're through feeling guilty, we'd better bury Hoke."

Whispering Jack's eyes were like ice daggers.

"What do you mean?"

"You think you could have done something to keep Katy O'Keefe and Nellie Bond alive. The fact is, you kind of liked the idea of Ronan being blackmailed. You wanted to see him squirm. You thought he'd pay up. But you misjudged him, and those two women are dead, and I don't think you could have saved them, anyway, so let's get on with it."

Capehart stared at him for what seemed to Torn like a small eternity. Torn couldn't help but wonder if Whispering Jack was going to take offense and try to kill him on the spot. The man had that kind of reputation.

Finally, Capehart stood up, took a deep breath, and instead of going for his gun, went to find a shovel.

They buried Hoke down near the river. When they were finished, Capehart leaned a while on his shovel and gazed up through the trees. The rain had stopped, and the summer sun was beating the clouds into fast-moving fragments.

"Someone once said that, like the sun, death can't be looked at steadily."

"It's done," said Torn. "Can't be undone. The dead are dead. You've got to take care of the living."

"Yeah. Fine." Capehart's whisper was harsh. "Let's go take care of some of the living who shouldn't be."

CHAPTER

31

TORN TOOK CREED'S SADDLE OFF THE DEAD HORSE AND
put it on a stodgy old mare in the corral behind the cabin.
The mare looked like she was more accustomed to the
trace, but she didn't kick up a fuss when Torn cinched the
hull on her back and put the bridle over her head.

He found some rope and a few pieces of warped planking
in a lean-to attached to the side of the cabin. Capehart
helped him tie a plank to Creed's back. They put the dead
man in his saddle and lashed him to it.

"I don't know," said Whispering Jack, standing back to
study their handiwork. "Close up, he looks downright
dead."

Torn had explained his plan to Capehart as they worked.
Now he said, "When they get that close it'll be too late."

"For them or us?"

They mounted up and rode through the trees in the
direction of the California Trail. Torn led the mare carrying

Creed. After a while he was satisfied that the corpse was going to stay upright in the saddle. The body slumped forward, head lolling, and the ropes that kept it in place were obvious, but Torn didn't think that mattered. He was betting that Ronan's men had orders to shoot first and ask questions later.

Of course, that was assuming Ronan's men would intercept them before they reached North Fork Town. And if they didn't? Torn tried not to dwell on that possibility.

Ronan had never trusted Creed. That much was clear. He couldn't be sure that Creed wouldn't turn against him. He would assume that if Torn was willing to risk returning to North Fork Town, he was returning with evidence.

When they reached the California Trail, Torn was still trying to convince himself that Ronan would act. If he did, it was tantamount to an admission of guilt. If he didn't— if he had the nerve to sit back and call the bluff—Torn would lose.

It was that simple. Torn had the answers, but no proof. Quite possibly, he would face a sentence of death for the murder of Spanish Red.

They turned east on the trail, a wide ribbon of red mud winding through rugged hills. The slopes were choked with brush and cluttered with rock outcroppings. *If they come*, wondered Torn, *will it be a face-to-face confrontation, or will they lurk in ambush?* His eyes, as gray and cold as gunmetal, ceaselessly scanned the hillsides.

It wasn't far to town; a handful of miles. Plenty of time had elapsed for Angevine to get to Long and for the word to reach Ronan, and for Ronan to make his play. So where the hell were they? Setting the pace, Torn held his horse to a walk. With every step the animal took, Torn's misgivings intensified. He was wound up tighter than an eight-day clock. In all his life he had never ached so badly for a fight.

And when it came, he was so relieved he laughed out loud.

The road curled around the shoulder of a hill, and as they made the bend they saw nine riders coming toward them. The nine checked their horses. So did Torn and Capehart. When Torn laughed, Whispering Jack gave him a funny look.

"You must be a real hardcase, Torn," said Capehart. "The odds don't bother you?"

Torn shook his head. "I never let them. You?"

Capehart grinned. "Modesty prevents me from answering."

Creed Walker's pistol rode in Torn's holster. He drew it, and the Spencer from the saddle boot. Both guns were fully loaded. Torn counted his rounds: six in the pistol, eight in the carbine. Capehart brandished his Dance revolver. Thirty yards away, the nine riders were filling their hands with shooting iron. Torn let go of the reins to Creed's horse.

For a moment frozen with tension, the only sound was the clack and clatter of rifle actions being worked, sidegun hammers being cocked, the rattle of bit chains, and the creak of saddle leather. A horse whickered.

Torn used the momentary standoff to evaluate his adversaries. He assumed they were all on the payroll of the Osage Trading Company. Engaged in criminal activity, Ronan would not likely employ cowards or gentlemen. These nine had the look of tough customers. *Probably not professional gunmen*, mused Torn, *but game enough for this kind of action*. He wondered if their pockets were heavy with gold double eagles, same as the men he and

Whispering Jack had killed in the shootout in town the other day.

"What are they waiting for?" asked Capehart. He sounded curious, not worried.

"Who knows," said Torn. His blood was up—that rush of exhilaration he'd felt time and time again during the war as he led his cavalry unit charging through the enemy. "Let's take it to 'em," he yelled.

Reins in his teeth, he kicked the horse into a gallop.

His first shot winged one of the Osage men, knocking him out of the saddle.

That broke the ice. The other eight spurred their mounts forward, yelling and shooting. Yellow spurts of gun-flame pierced a sudden fog of white powdersmoke. Hot lead shimmied in the air. Torn was dimly aware of Capehart galloping right alongside, the Dance booming.

Slamming right into the charge of the Osage men, Torn fired point-blank into the chest of one foe. The man somersaulted over the back of his running horse. Screaming like a banshee, a man on the other side of Torn aimed his pistol at Torn's head and pulled the trigger. Looking down the barrel, Torn felt his heart stop. In that split second, with excruciating clarity, he watched the hammer drop, and knew he was dead.

The gun misfired.

Torn's horse, still galloping, carried him on by. He threw a shot over his shoulder without really aiming, then pulled the trigger again. The pistol clicked empty. He threw it away, snatched the reins out of his teeth, and checked and turned the horse.

Six Osage men were still mounted. Five of them were wrangling their horses around to face Torn. The sixth galloped on down the road. The horse carrying Creed Walker had veered off into the brush, and the sixth rider was going after him. Torn figured they had orders to make sure Creed didn't reach North Fork Town alive. Little did they know that Torn had settled that himself.

As Capehart turned his horse, the first man Torn had shot came up out of the mud and fired at Whispering Jack. He missed the man, killed the horse. Capehart jumped clear, the Dance revolver spitting .44 caliber death into the man's face. He whirled, took a few blind, staggering steps, then pitched forward.

The rest of Ronan's hirelings were charging again. Torn sent two more rounds into them, without apparent effect. His horse was prancing and sidestepping, making accurate shooting virtually impossible. He heeled the animal into a jumping-start gallop and headed straight into the midst of the enemy. He got off one more shot and saw a man tumble from the saddle. Then his horse collided head-on with another. Both horses went down, both men were unseated. Torn plowed into the mud, scrambling to get clear of flailing hooves. The three Osage men still mounted thundered past. The one Torn had run into was getting to his feet, dazed. Torn jammed the barrel of the Spencer into his gut and pulled the trigger. The impact of the bullet lifted him off his feet and hurled him backwards. He slid twenty feet in the muck, and was dead before he came to a stop.

Torn's horse was getting back up. He vaulted into the saddle, grabbing for rein leather. A sudden jolt of white hot pain wrenched a gasp out of him. The pain, in his left arm, was immediately followed by a cold numbness. He'd been shot, but he didn't let it rattle him. He got the horse under control, turned it.

Capehart was taking on the three Osage riders. Gun thunder bounced off the rocky hillsides on either side. Torn heard another gun join in behind him. He twisted in the saddle. The man who had chased after Creed was coming up the road to rejoin the fray. Torn took careful aim and squeezed the trigger. The man's rebel yell ended abruptly with a shriek of pain. He pitched sideways off his mount.

Looking back toward the duel between Capehart and the other Osage men, Torn saw Whispering Jack account for one of his foes before going down in a spinning fall. The two remaining Osage men rode on up the trail a ways before pulling up and looking back. They hesitated, taking stock of their losses and the situation, reloading their guns. Sparing Capehart a quick glance, Torn detected no signs of life. Whispering Jack was a crumpled, mud-splattered heap.

Again clenching the reins in his teeth, Torn braced the Spencer against his shoulder and fired at the two men. He missed. They wheeled and charged. He goaded his own horse forward. A bullet sang past Torn's ear. Another grazed his leg. His last bullet punched one of the Osage riders in the chest. He slipped out of the saddle. His boot snagged in the stirrup. The horse galloped on, dragging the dead man, whose body laid a deep furrow in the mud of the California Trail.

Torn heard the Spencer dry-fire. As he and the last Osage rider closed, he swung the empty carbine like a club. The Osage man fired. Torn felt the impact, like someone hitting him in the hip with an ax handle. The Spencer's barrel smashed the Osage man squarely in the face. He rolled off the back of his horse and landed spread-eagled in the mud.

Checking and turning the horse, Torn saw the man roll over, drooling blood. Torn dismounted, walked over, and came within range as the man struggled to his feet, reeling, his face a scarlet mask of rage. Torn recognized him then—

this was the one he had seen leaving Spanish Red's last night.

The man whipped a knife out of his belt and lunged. Torn swung the Spencer. The carbine's stock shattered against the man's shoulder, hammering him to the ground. The knife went flying. Casting away the ruined Spencer, Torn retrieved the knife. The man was up on his hands and knees now, head lolling. Torn kicked him in the side. He fell over on his back. A knee in the man's chest, Torn put the blade against his throat.

"Live or die," rasped Torn. "It's up to you."

All the fight went out of the man. "Don't kill me."

Torn pulled the man to his feet, walked him over to Capehart's dead horse, and ordered him to sit down with his hands behind him. The man complied, and Torn tied his hands securely with the dead animal's reins.

Ears ringing with the echo of gun thunder, Torn stood there a moment, surveying the carnage. Ten men lay dead or dying in the red mud. Riderless horses were scattering. Far off down the road, Creed's horse was trotting away, carrying its dead cargo.

Torn checked himself for damage. His left sleeve was slick with blood, but he hadn't lost the use of the arm. He searched for the source of the pain lancing through his hip. No wound. Reaching into the pocket of his frock coat, he pulled out Big Mike Walker's badge. The bullet had turned it into a piece of mangled steel.

He remembered that night in the jailhouse with Big Mike's bullet-riddled body laid out on the desk, when Long had placed the badge in his keeping. Torn couldn't say why he hadn't worn the badge pinned to his shirt in the customary manner. But he was sure of one thing: God had a habit of looking out for the foolhardy.

As he slogged through the mire toward Whispering Jack

he got a pleasant surprise. Capehart moved, moaned, and sat up slowly. The bullet had laid a deep furrow across his temple. Blood covered the side of his face and neck.

"A hair closer and you'd be buzzard bait," said Torn.

"Can't be that I've been living right."

The sound of horses coming fast galvanized Torn. The trail was strewn with weapons, and he dived for the nearest one, a Winchester "Yellow Boy" repeater. He jacked a round into the breech and stood ready as another bunch of riders appeared from the direction of North Fork Town.

CHAPTER

32

IN THE MIDST OF THE SIX HORSEMEN WAS A BUCKBOARD
pulled by a team of mules. Long Walker rode in the bed
of the wagon on blanket-covered straw.

The six riders, realized Torn, were Creeks from town,
and he wondered if any of them had been in the mob bent
on lynching him the night before.

Returning to his prisoner, Torn used the man's knife to
cut the reins, and walked him over to the wagon.

"Is Angevine safe?" he asked Long.

The Creek elder nodded. "She wanted to come along.
I told her no. She waits for you in town."

"This is one of Ronan's men," said Torn. "Ronan sent
him and these others to stop me."

Long looked impassively at the bodies in the mud.

"And Creed?"

"Dead," said Torn. "I killed him. I persuaded Angevine
to lie to you about that. Don't blame her."

Long nodded at the news of Creed's death, his face betraying none of the emotion twisting inside him. Torn got the impression that Long had already known, somehow, that Creed was dead.

Capehart staggered to the wagon, reloading his Dance revolver, as Torn said, "This is one of the men who framed me for the murder of Spanish Red. He wants to tell you all about it."

But the Osage man had a case of cold feet. He shook his head stubbornly.

"I ain't got nothing to say."

Capehart pushed Torn aside. Slamming the Osage man against the wagon, he cocked the Dance and planted the barrel against the prisoner's head.

"Then there's no point in a useless son-of-a-bitch like you breathing good air," snarled Whispering Jack.

The Osage man's new-found courage vanished like a dead fire's ashes in a strong wind.

"Awright!" he bawled. "I'll talk. I was at Spanish Red's last night. Me and that yellowleg sergeant, Jurgen. It was Jurgen pistol-whipped you, Judge. We carried you back into Red's. Jurgen took your knife and killed her. When he made Red write that letter, he told her it was you we were gonna kill. I didn't know it was a frame-up, as God is my witness. Mr. Ronan ordered me to go along and help Jurgen, that's all."

"Just like he ordered you and your friends to ride out and kill me," said Torn.

The man nodded, sweating fear. "You and Creed Walker."

"Where's Ronan?" growled Capehart.

The man shrugged, too scared to speak further.

"I figure he's waiting in North Fork Town," said Torn. "He didn't have the guts to come do his own killing."

"Let's go," said Capehart. "He owes on a debt."

"He is dead," said Long.

Capehart stared at the old Creek as though he had suddenly lost the ability to comprehend the English language.

"Dead?" echoed Torn, his voice hollow.

"Angevine told me what you said about Ronan and Creed smuggling guns to our enemies, the Kiowas and Comanches. I sent a man to watch Ronan's house. I wondered what he would do when he heard you were bringing Creed to me. When the man I sent got to his house, Ronan's wife came running out into the street. She discovered her husband's body in his study. His throat had been cut."

Stunned, Capehart staggered away from the wagon. Torn watched him go. He felt sorry for Whispering Jack. Capehart had hoped to ease the burden of guilt he carried for the deaths of Katy O'Keefe and Nellie Bond—deaths he might have been able to prevent—by killing Ronan. It wouldn't have worked, of course; revenge never did. But Torn didn't bother trying to explain that to him.

When he turned back to Long, Torn saw his saber-knife in the Creek elder's hands. Long held the weapon out for him to take, but Torn hesitated. The image of the saber-knife buried to the hilt in Spanish Red haunted him.

"This man Jurgen," said Long. "He must have killed Ronan."

Torn nodded. "I reckon you could say the thieves had a falling out. That's what happens when you lie down with mad dogs. You get bit."

"Ronan's wife said her husband's strongbox is missing from his desk. Jurgen probably took it. He must be halfway out of the Creek Nation by now."

Torn grimly took the saber-knife and secured it in the shoulder rig under his coat.

"I didn't think he'd leave without settling with me. But that's all right. I'll just have to go after him."

The dawn accompanied Long Walker into North Fork Town. He trudged up the Texas Road, his movements stiff with age and arthritis, and he relied on his hickory cane as he navigated the wide expanse of rutted dust.

As he stepped out of the stone jailhouse, Torn saw the old Creek coming. A saddled horse—the dun gelding he had purchased at John Eagle's livery—was hitched to the tie rail. Torn slid his Winchester .44–40 into the saddle boot. In his holster was the Colt .45 Peacemaker he had recovered from the Osage man captured in the fight yesterday. Torn hadn't known it then, but the man had been trying to kill him with his own gun. He was glad to get the Peacemaker back; in his opinion it was the most reliable sidegun available.

The saber-knife rode in its shoulder rig under the black frock coat cleaned and mended last night by Angevine, while Doc Crane had tended to Torn's injuries. The bullet had gone through his arm, missing the bone. The dressing bulked beneath his sleeve, and the wound throbbed with a dull, relentless pain. Crane had advised him against riding for a few days, but Torn was leaving North Fork Town this morning.

When Long arrived, Torn bade him good morning. "I'm glad you came by. I wanted to say so long, and give you this."

He took the bullet-maimed badge out of his pocket and put it in Long's hand.

"You are going after Jurgen," said Long.

Torn nodded. "You said it yourself. A warm trail is easier to follow."

"Where will you start?"

"Fort Gibson. Might get some idea from the soldiers there where he'd run to."

"And if no one there can help?"

"The Unassigned Lands, I reckon."

Long glanced at the door to the jailhouse. "Angevine?"

Torn grimaced. "She's inside. Sleeping."

The old Creek's dark, piercing eyes seemed to bore right through Torn.

"If you're wondering whether anything happened between us," said Torn, acutely uncomfortable, "it didn't. After the doc finished with me—and after I finished a bottle of Old Crow from the French Lily—I was dead to the world. When I woke up this morning, I found her sleeping in a chair."

"I wasn't wondering," said Long, the hint of a smile touching his lips.

"Well, just in case you were," said Torn, cross with himself. He drew a ragged breath and let it out slowly. "Damn it, Long," he whispered. "If anything happened, I don't think I would ever leave."

Long nodded and put a sympathetic hand on Torn's shoulder. "I will tell her goodbye for you."

Torn glanced at the jailhouse door, feeling guilty. Guilty about leaving Angevine this way, slipping away like a coward. Guilty about his feelings for her, equating those feelings with being unfaithful to Melony Hancock. He wondered if he was making the wrong decision a second time.

The Texas Road was not yet teeming with life. The sound of a horse and buggy coming from the north drew Torn's attention. Whispering Jack Capehart, hatless, with a dressing around his head, was driving. A woman rode beside him. She wore a somber black dress. Her raven-black hair was done up beneath a small hat, from which depended a veil concealing her features.

As the buggy passed the jailhouse, Capehart glanced at Torn. He smiled faintly, almost apologetically. The woman did not turn her head. The buggy rolled on. Torn stared after it.

"Who was that with Capehart?" he asked Long.

"Elizabeth Ronan," answered Long, and Torn detected disapproval in the Creek elder's voice. "Her husband was buried at dawn."

Long volunteered no more in the way of explanation. Torn didn't need any help figuring it out. The last piece of the puzzle fell into place.

Now he understood Capehart's stab at respectability, why he had stopped seeing Katy O'Keefe. His interest had been focused on someone else. Torn remembered Ronan saying *she hasn't behaved like a wife for quite some time. She doesn't have anything to do with me.* That much, then, had been true. Torn was willing to bet she had fallen hard for the dashing Whispering Jack.

"I hope they'll be happy together," he murmured.

Long gave him a curious look, not knowing whether Torn was being sincere or sardonic.

Torn shook the old Creek's hand. "Goodbye, Long."

"Maybe one day you will come back this way."

"Maybe," said Torn, climbing aboard the dun gelding, knowing in his heart he would swing a wide loop around North Fork Town henceforth, for his own peace of mind, and for Angevine's sake.

Long turned away and retraced his steps down the Texas Road. Torn watched him for a moment. His heart went out to the old man. Long had no family left. Torn knew how lonely that could be. Then he reminded himself that all the Creeks revered Long Walker. The Nation was his family.

Sparing the jailhouse a last, pensive glance, Torn neck-reined the horse and headed north.

"Clay!"

Torn checked the dun sharply and turned in the saddle. Angevine emerged from the jailhouse. She ran after him.

At that moment a man stepped out of the alley adjacent to the jailhouse.

Jurgen.

He'd exchanged his uniform for civilian clothes, and wore a yellow duster. A slouch hat was pulled down low over his face. His bristled cheek bulged with a quid of tobacco. He still wore cavalry boots, and the army-issue belt and holster. The holster was empty, though—the revolver was in his hand.

"Angevine, look out!" yelled Torn.

Angevine's appearance threw Jurgen off. He fired at Torn—a second too late. Torn was already hurling himself sideways off the horse. He hit the ground on his wounded arm and almost blacked out from the pain. He rolled instinctively. Jurgen got off a second shot. The bullet spewed dirt into Torn's eyes. Torn groped for the Colt at his hip. Angevine stood in the middle of the road, directly in the line of fire.

"Get down!" he bellowed.

Realizing he had lost the element of surprise, Jurgen lunged for Angevine. Torn dragged the Colt clear of holster leather, but he didn't have time to get off a shot. Jurgen grabbed Angevine roughly and held her in front of him as a human shield, his gun to her head.

"Drop the iron, Judge!"

Torn was up on one knee now. He didn't hesitate, tossed the Colt away.

Jurgen's grin was an ugly sight.

"You didn't think I'd head for the hills without settlin'

with you first, did you, Judge?"

Torn stood, moving slowly. "I was hoping you wouldn't."
He took a step closer. Jurgen responded by pressing the
gun harder against Angevine's head. Her eyes were riv-
eted to Torn. She was afraid—afraid for him. And Torn
was afraid for her. She was at the mercy of a man who
killed because he enjoyed killing.

"It's me you want," said Torn harshly. "Let her go."

"I think I'll kill her right in front of your eyes. How about
that, Judge?"

"You afraid of me, Jurgen?" Torn held his arms out away
from his sides. "I'm unarmed. Why are you afraid of me?"

"I'm not afraid of you, you bastard," sneered Jurgen.

Torn took another step. He had to get closer. He
couldn't swallow the lump in his throat; he could scarcely
breathe. He had never felt so helpless. Somehow he had
to save Angevine. But how? He was convinced Jurgen
would kill her just for the hell of it.

"You're a coward, Jurgen," he said. "Why are you hiding
behind a woman?"

Somehow, thought Torn, *I have to take that first bullet.*
He was focused on Jurgen, and only vaguely aware of
people appearing up and down the street. If he could take
that first bullet, maybe, just maybe, Angevine had a slim
chance. Maybe someone else would kill Jurgen before he
could turn the gun back on her. A thousand-to-one odds,
but Torn couldn't see any other way.

"Come on, coward," he sneered. "Shoot me, you yellow
bastard. Can't do it, can you?"

"Shut up!" yelled Jurgen, hoarse.

"You can't do it," said Torn, derisive. "You can't look
a man straight in the eyes and kill him. You backshot
Rutledge. You slipped up behind Ronan, didn't you? It's
only defenseless women you can kill face to face. You're

the sorriest excuse for a . . ."

Jurgen uttered a hoarse, incoherent yell of pure rage. He swung the gun at Torn. Angevine had been trying to pry his arm from around her waist. Now she reached up and struck his gunarm just as he fired. Torn didn't know if he actually felt the breath of the bullet or if it was just his imagination. As he lunged the last ten feet, his hand streaked under his frock coat. He thumbed the leather thong off the pommel of the saber-knife. The saber-knife slid out of the sheath strapped upside-down against his ribcage, into his hand. He plowed into Angevine and Jurgen. All three went down in a tangle. Jurgen fired again as he fell, purely by reflex, and the shot went wild. He slipped out of Torn's grasp and scrambled away. Torn pushed Angevine flat on the ground and went after him. As Jurgen turned, leveling the gun, Torn hit him square-on, driving him into the wall of the jailhouse, grabbing the barrel and wrenching it downward as the gun went off, driving the saber-knife into Jurgen's belly and ripping savagely downward.

As he held Jurgen pinned to the wall, staring into the sergeant's eyes, watching the man die, Torn felt his own body go cold. His blood seemed to turn to ice. For one brief, nightmarish instant, he saw Karl Schmidt's face. The way he had last seen it, contorted in agony, as Torn cut him open with his own saber.

Then Jurgen convulsed, drooled blood, and died.

Torn stepped back, wrenching the knife free and letting Jurgen fall. He bent, wiping the blade of the saber-knife on the dead man's duster. As he turned, Angevine confronted him.

"Are you all right?" he asked.

She nodded, reached out to him. "Clay . . ."

"I can't stay, Angevine. I've got a job to do."

"And when it's over?"

He glanced at Jurgen's corpse.

"It may never be over. Don't waste any more of your life waiting for me."

The dun gelding stood in the Texas Road. As he headed for the horse, Torn sheathed the saber-knife and retrieved his Colt. People were gathering around the jailhouse, coming from all directions. He was aware, without looking straight at them, of Long Walker standing with Angevine.

He mounted up and rode out of North Fork Town without once looking back. His attention was fixed on the road that lay before him. He wondered when it would lead him to Melony, and how many Karl Schmidts he would run into along the way.